THE BEAR HUNTERS

Dave Larson

PublishAmerica
Baltimore

© 2007 by Dave Larson.
All rights reserved. No part of this book may be reproduced, stored in a retrieval system or transmitted in any form or by any means without the prior written permission of the publishers, except by a reviewer who may quote brief passages in a review to be printed in a newspaper, magazine or journal.

All characters in this book are fictitious, and any resemblance to real persons, living or dead, is coincidental.

First printing

At the specific preference of the author, PublishAmerica allowed this work to remain exactly as the author intended, verbatim, without editorial input.

ISBN: 1-4241-6835-X
PUBLISHED BY PUBLISHAMERICA, LLLP
www.publishamerica.com
Baltimore

Printed in the United States of America

To:

Pat, my wife and encourager

Brant, my friend and mentor

Prologue

The Bear

It was during that time of year when the wind turned cold, and the interior Alaskan hillsides became aflame with the colors of red and yellow. Quaking aspen trees shivered as if they were chilled. Bright red blueberry bushes were laden with fruit as far as the eye could see.

In a small valley, about a hundred miles southwest of Fairbanks, a large grizzly bear was stuffing himself with berries, mice, grubs, roots and anything else he deemed edible. He was doing what his ancestors had been doing for thousands of generations, fattening himself for a long winter's night.

He was a large male, weighing about 800 pounds. He could stand to a full eight feet in height. His lineage stretched from Siberia where his ancestors crossed the Bering land bridge, along with mammoths and Inuits. His coat was yellow brown, changing to almost black at the paws. Some of the hairs on his fur were tipped with white giving him a grizzled look. Each paw had claws six to eight inches long, and used to provide food by ripping grubs out of logs, or to dig the ground to make a den. They were also formidable weapons when confronted by another grizzly. He had a large muscular hump high on his back, across the shoulders, giving him the power to dig. He had a keen nose and acute hearing. Normally, he would stay out of the way of humans, but not always. If he had to defend himself, he could live up to his Latin name, "Ursus Arctos Horribilis," Horrible Arctic Bear.

Outside of Man, the Grizzly Bear is one of the most dangerous animals on the planet. It is also one of the most intelligent. They have been known to track down and kill the very hunters trying to kill them. They've followed a man's scent to his cabin, ripped off the door and shredded the hapless occupants.

A bear is like any other wild animal. It does whatever its species are programmed to do, from day to day, season to season, and year to year. There is no awareness of right or wrong, love or hate, or any other feeling not needed to procreate and survive. What is a bear's purpose? Whatever is God's pleasure.

It was time to make his hibernation den. He walked to a slight upward slope covered with large rocks. At the base of the rocks he dug into the slope until he had made a tunnel with a sleeping chamber at its end. The soil he pulled out of the cave was heaped into a mound around the opening. Then, he entered the chamber for the last time, settled in and went to sleep.

The snows came and covered the ground and the mound over the den. The nights grew longer. The Northern Lights flashed across the sky like huge glowing curtains. They were always in motion, and it appeared snow flakes were being shaken from the creases of its fabric. The beauty of nature was all around, but no one was there to see.

Johnny D'Angelo

On the Streets

Johnny D'Angelo was a product of the slums of Brooklyn, New York. He and his four brothers and two sisters were raised by their mother, who would do anything to put food on the table. Like his sibs, Johnny had no idea who his father was. He had no one to teach him how to defend himself, and just about every day he went to school he was challenged. It was all part of the social system for the boys to be ranked by how tough they were. He wasn't as big as many of them, so he always got trounced. He knew life was never going to get better unless he could win a few fights. He had to figure a way to raise himself from the bottom of the totem.

There was an unwritten system of rules of engagement. For one thing, a kid was always challenged to a fight by some insulting words like, "Your mother's a whore!" That would almost always start a fight. But, still there were some kids that were just afraid and wouldn't do anything. According to the unwritten rules, there was no point in just beating someone who wouldn't defend himself.

This gave Johnny an idea. Suppose instead of waiting for someone to challenge him, he would be proactive and start a fight. To improve his chances of winning, he had to be sure to pick a kid who was afraid to fight. To make the right impression, he thought he should pick the largest kid. A fat Jewish kid came to mind, Harold Fishman.

He had his target picked, now what? Don't give the kid a chance to decline. Just tear into him. If the kid hollers he gives up, don't let him go until he's totally beaten. Johnny could hardly wait to try out his plan.

The next day at recess when the kids were on the playground, Johnny walked up to Harold and shouted for all to hear, "Hey, Fishman! Your mother's a whore!" Before Harold had a chance to run away, Johnny slugged him in the face. The kid went down screaming, while Johnny kept pummeling him. Pretty soon Harold's face was a mass of blood, snot and dirt. All of the other kids standing there were speechless. The playground teacher pulled him off of the poor kid, and took him to the principal's office. Johnny was expelled for a few days, and when he came back to school, he found he was number one on the totem. The other boys were afraid of him, and he kept them terrorized.

He quit school when he was twelve, and worked the streets by stealing and making some of the local kids pay him weekly "protection money," for not beating them up.

For five years he was successful in bringing home some money for his mother. Then his mother got sick with pneumonia and died. His sisters left with boyfriends, and his brothers disappeared. Johnny had no idea where they went, and didn't care.

Someone noticed him, and one day he was approached by a suave young man in his twenties. Johnny was on his usual street corner with some of his friends when the man walked up to him.

"Hi, kid," the man said.

Johnny looked at the coolest guy he'd ever seen. The man's shoes were shined to a mirror finish, and his clothes were tailored to fit like a glove. He wore expensive sunglasses, a broad brimmed hat and a disarming smile.

"Hi," responded Johnny, totally absorbed in a vision of what he hoped would be himself someday.

"My name's Dino, but my friends call me Wop," said the man. "What's your name, kid?" asked Dino and at the same time giving Johnny's friends a "get lost" look.

"My name's Johnny. Johnny D'Angelo," he answered warily.

"Ya know, Johnny, this is your lucky day."

"Yeah?"

"Yeah. I've been watching you. You're pretty good with your fists, ain't ya?"

"Yeah. Maybe."

"How would ya like to learn how to really fight?"

"Wadda ya mean?" asked Johnny.

"I mean, how'd ya like to take boxing lessons in a real gym?"

"You're just playing wit' me. How can I do dat?"

"I mean it. I'll pay for it," said Dino, as he watched the expression on Johnny's face change from puzzlement to surprise.

"Ya mean you'd just give me the money for da lessons?"

"Well, not exactly. You'd be earning the money by working for me," said Dino as he carefully snared Johnny.

He looked Dino in the face, and then asked, "Wadda I gotta do?"

"Same as you're doin' now, collectin' money," said Dino as he flashed his white teeth with a smile.

"I don't get it," said Johnny.

"Well, here's the thing. Yer freelancing right now. Ain't that right?"

"Is dat wha'ch ya call it?"

"Yeah, that's what I call it."

"OK, den. I'm freelancin'."

"Do ya make any money?"

"Maybe five or six dollars on some days. Maybe nothing on other days."

"I'll pay you twenty five dollars a week and take care of your gym fees."

Johnny couldn't believe what he heard.

"When do I start, man?"

"Wop. My friends call me Wop. How 'bout startin' right now?"

Dino pulled out his wallet and peeled off a twenty and a five and gave it to him.

"This is yer signin' bonus. I'll give ya another twenty-five in a week."

"Wow! T'anks! T'anks a lot!"

"C'mon, Johnny. My car's over here. Let's drive to the gym and get started."

An Opportunity

Dino led Johnny up the street about a block to a beautiful new two-door Caddy convertible. The body of the car was custom painted to a bright reddish orange and the top was an ivory white, as was the upholstery. The car was clean and polished with no scuff marks on the whitewall tires.

"Dis' is yer car?" asked Johnny, without taking his eyes off of it.

"Yep. Do ya like it?"

"Man, I'll say. People can see ya comin' wit' dis."

"That's one of the reasons I chose the color. I'm in the lendin' business. My clients can see me when I'm in the 'hood."

Before they climbed into the car, Dino checked Johnny's pockets to make sure he had no sharp objects that might damage the upholstery.

"This is my pride and joy, Johnny. Be real careful getting in and out."

"Right, Boss."

"It's OK to call me Wop, Johnny. We're friends."

Johnny felt funny calling him, Wop. That was one of his fighting words.

"OK, Wop," he finally said.

Dino started the Caddy and smoothly pulled out into traffic. They had only traveled about a mile when he stopped in front of a rundown warehouse. It was in an old deserted part of town. All of the wooden buildings looked the same, brown with age and in need of repair and paint. The lower windows had bars that were covered over with sheet metal. Most of the upper windows were broken out, probably by kids with slingshots or BB guns.

"Doesn't look like much from the outside," said Dino "but, it's a gym and Joey's a good trainer."

Dino opened the glove box and fished out a bundle of keys. He sorted through them until he found the one he wanted and took it off of the ring. He palmed the key in his hand and they exited the car. Johnny followed him as he walked to a locked wooden door on the front of the building. He opened the deadbolt with his key, and they entered.

"Wow," said Johnny, as he took in the surroundings.

In the middle of the big room, he saw a brightly lit boxing ring where a couple of guys were sparring. Around the ring were lighted stations where people were working out on punching bags, sandbags, rope-jumping and bodybuilding equipment. He was surprised to even see a couple of women working out.

"Dis place is fantastic!" said Johnny as they walked toward the boxing ring.

"Why's it so dark in here, Wop?"

"'Cause the windows are boarded up, and they put lights only where people work out."

"Why not light up da whole room?"

"Too expensive. Unless yer gonna raise pot," said Dino with a grin.

Dino always had an answer for Johnny's questions. Some of his answers were even truthful, but many were not. The real reason the ring and workout stations were brightly lit and in the center of the room, was to keep eyes from being seen as they watched and appraised the action.

"Hey, Joey!" hollered Dino as he greeted a frumpy, slightly balding, middle aged man sitting at a table next to the ring.

"Hey, Wop! How ya doin'?" replied Joey, as he stood up to shake hands.

"Doin' great, my man! Hey, I want ya to meet my new friend, Johnny."

"Hi, Johnny," said Joey with a friendly smile as he extended his right arm.
"Hi," replied, Johnny, shaking his hand.
"So, ya wanna be a fighter?"
"Yeah."
"He's already pretty good, Joey," added Dino.
"All right, ya see dat man over there?" said Joey, pointing.
"Yeah," responded Johnny.
"He's the equipment manager. His name's Donny. You tell him I said to fix you up. He'll give you everything you need, including a locker and a key to the entrance door."
"Okay!" said Johnny as he ran off.
"Seems like a nice kid," reflected Joey.
"Looks can be deceiving," replied Dino as they watched Donny take the kid under his wing.
"How's dat?"
"When I found him, he was running his own protection racket."
"No kiddin'! With the knuckles an' all?"
"Yep. I think this one will work out pretty well."
Dino meant Johnny might show some early promise. Most of the kids Dino brought in were rejected early in their training program.
At first Dino hated this part of his job, but then got over it. When one of his boys didn't pass muster with Dino's boss, he'd have to drive the kid to some remote place, take his key away from him, and then beat him senseless.
"You ever talk to anyone about our business, I'll come back and kill ya," he would say.
He would then abandon the poor kid by driving off.
Joey couldn't understand how Dino could be so friendly to the boys one minute and then so brutal the next.
"You get pretty tight with these kids, don't ya?"
"Sure. I can sympathize with 'em. This is about their only chance to get outta the 'hood."
"So how can ya fire 'em and put the shoes to 'em?"
"My mom taught me."

"Really? How's dat?"

"When I was growin' up, my family lived outside of the city where it was okay to keep chickens. My mom raised them for the eggs we'd sell. The hens were just like pets. She'd give them names, and they'd come when ya called them. I use to pet 'em and feed 'em scratch outta my hand. But, if one quit layin' eggs, my mom would pick her up and start talkin' to her.

"She'd say, 'Why, Biddy, why aren't you layin' eggs? I'm sorry, Biddy.'

"Then she'd take the hen to a choppin' block. She'd take up the hatchet that was stuck into the wood, and gently laid the hen's neck across the top of the block.

"Whack!

"The head would fly in one direction, and the rest of the chicken would fly off in the other. And I mean fly. That headless chicken would flap its wings and actually lift off the ground.

"I asked my mom, 'How can you do this? I thought you loved your chickens.'

"Then she said, 'I do love them. They're my pets. But, I've got a business arrangement with them. If they don't produce, I can't afford to keep them, so they go into the pot. I'm not mad at them. It's just the way life is.'"

"But, why do ya have to beat up the kids?" asked Joey.

"D'Vito would prefer I kill them, but I can't do that. So I do the next best thing to make sure they don't tell anyone about our business. If word would ever get out about his involvement in this gym, we'd have to shut down the program and I'd get whacked."

Donny brought Johnny back to where the two men were standing.

"Well, he's all set. He put all of the stuff in his locker."

"What kind a schedule you want for him, Wop?" asked Joey.

"How about you spending a couple hours a morning coaching him, and I'll spend some time with him in the afternoon? When we're not with him, he can work out on the equipment."

"You gonna teach me boxing too, Wop?"

"Well, Joey's gonna teach ya how to box, I'm gonna teach ya how to help me collect debts."

Dino Has a Bad Day

Johnny began his training with flair. He couldn't get enough of it. Then, one afternoon, only a couple of weeks into the program, Joey had some words with Dino while Johnny worked in the ring.

"Hey, Wop. Have you been watchin' dis kid spar?"

"Sort of. What's the matter?"

Joey took a long draw on his cigarette he usually had dangling from his lower lip.

"He's not pullin' his punches. He's tryin' to kill his sparrin' partner. Some of 'em won't get in da ring wit' him anymore."

"Did ya talk to him?"

"It don't do no good. He's an arrogant little bastard. Why don't you try talkin' to him?"

Just then, the door to the street opened. The light it emitted was blinding as it reflect off of the snow outside. Dino and Joey saw four men enter the room, all bundled in their thick overcoats. Although he couldn't see their faces, he knew one of them was his boss.

"Oh, jeez. They're lookin' over Johnny," said Dino fearfully.

After the door closed, the intruders disappeared into the darkness of the outer edge of the room. Just as Joey and Dino turned their attention back to the ring there was a loud *wham, bang,* and *thud,* as Johnny knocked-out his sparring partner.

Oh, no! thought Dino, *D'Vito's gonna kill me!*

Joey's cigarette was now so short he burned his fingers trying to get it out of his mouth.

One of the visitors walked up to Joey and spoke into his ear. He got up from his chair and followed the man back into the darkness. Dino was sweating, wondering if he was going to catch hell too. Then the outside door opened again and the four men left as Joey was returning to his chair. Dino wonder how bad the news was going to be.

Joey sat down and looked at Dino who couldn't wait for the words.
"Well?!"
Joey lit another cigarette and blew out a cloud of smoke.
"Dey asked me 'bout the kid."
"And?!"
"I tol' 'em he was a problem because I was runnin' outta sparrin' partners."
"Wha'd they say?!"
"D'Vito said to pay 'em more money so they'd get in the ring wit' him!"
"His money or yours?"
"His, I hope! I was afraid ta ask."

There were more surprise visits over the following months and assessments given to D'Vito by Joey. Then one day Dino got a call from his boss, who wanted to meet with him. Usually, Dino would get his orders by phone and would only see the boss in person if there were problems.

D'Vito's nickname was Dad, which was made from the initials of his full name, Dominic Angelo D'Vito. Dino always addressed his boss as, Dad. It had a family sound to it and suggested his boss was a benevolent and protective man, which he was neither, unless he benefited.

D'vito rose through the ranks, like Dino was trying to do, and commanded a fairly high position in the family. There was only one position between him and the top. He earned recognition and respect from those above him by his performance. The same was required for those below him. Performance was required at the costs of threats and violence.

A very anxious Dino arrived at his boss's office exactly on time. With hat in hand, he entered the inner office and faced D'Vito, who sat behind a massive desk.

"Good morning, Dad."

"Hello, Dino."

D'Vito looked like a middle-aged businessman. He was about average in height with a slim build. He wore dark brown slacks, with the tan sport coat, a white shirt, and a wide tie with brown and tan diagonal stripes. His trimmed black hair showed no signs of graying. He looked the essence of health, except he had to use reading glasses, which he referred to as "cheaters". He was cordial and smiled at Dino. But, in reality he was as dangerous as a coiled rattlesnake.

"Yer lookin' well Dad."

D'Vito brushed aside the condescending perfunctory remark and got down to business.

"I wanna talk about dis kid yer trainin' on my money."

"Hey, I'm really sorry about…"

D'Vito cut him off.

"Look, I t'ink da kid has promise. What were ya plannin' on doin' wit' him?"

"Well, he's a tough kid. I thought maybe he could make it as a boxer, and we could make some money off him."

"You plannin' on havin' 'im collect loans wit' you?"

"Well, yeah."

D'Vito pressed his hands together and paused in thought.

"Nah, don't do dat. I don't want anyt'ing ta happin' to him. I t'ink we'd do better to make a prize fighter outta him."

"Okay."

"Now, as for you, I'm not happy wit' yer performance. I t'ink yer too soft."

"Gee, Dad, I'm sorry…"

"Bein' sorry don't cut it. Now you stick wit' dat kid and make sure nuttin' bad happens to 'im. Let Joey make a boxer outta 'im. An' I want you to do a better job at collectin' on yer loans. Put some hurt on da freeloaders. *Capisce*??"

"But, Dad. Some of these guys are strung out and can't pay!"

Big mistake. Dino wished he could take those words back as he watched D'Vito's face turn to a bright crimson.

"Yer givin' my money to druggies!" D'Vito shouted as he stood up from his chair.

"Oh, please!" Dino prayed. *"Please let a bullet crash through the window and into his head! Or, even my head!"*

But, no matter how hard he prayed, no bullet came. The tirade went on and on as D'Vito screamed at Dino, calling him every insulting name he had ever heard, and some in Italian he hadn't heard before. It finally ended with,

"Now, get outta here!"

Dino left the room completely whipped. He felt trapped, and wished he'd finished college instead of ever getting into the business. Now he was in too deep, and few ever retired from the family other than permanently.

Johnny Becomes a Fighter

Time passes. Days become weeks, weeks become months, and Johnny became eighteen. He was impressive. Now, he was fighting for real. Joey contacted other fight managers and set up matches with their boys. None of them could stand up to Johnny more than three rounds before they were on the canvas. Not only could he hit hard, but he was fast. Dino stayed with him constantly, and they became great friends. Johnny was forever thanking him for helping to find his dream.

"Ya know, Wop, if it wasn't for you, I'd still be on the streets tryin' to run my two-bit racket."

He was now sharing Dino's apartment, and girls. He had a lot to be thankful for.

Dino was all smiles too.

"Well, you're the one doin' the hard work, Johnny. Maybe someday we can both get outta here."

Johnny was surprised.

"You mean ya don't like yer job, Wop?"

"I like workin' with you, Johnny, but I don't like the loan business."

"Why not?"

"I got into trouble with my boss for lending to deadbeats, so I'm tryin' to just keep the loans in the family, but some of these guys are just as bad."

"Ya need some help?"

"Nah, you stick to boxing."

They drove to the gym together, and Joey was waiting for them.

"Hey, Wop, I gotta talk to you guys."

They went into Joey's cramped office.

"What's up?" asked Dino.

"We've gone through all the available kids to fight, Johnny. I think it's time for him to take on a contender."

"Wow! What'd ya think of that, Johnny?"

"Hey, I'm ready!'

"Should I tell D'Vito, Joey?"

"No. Let's wait 'til after the first fight."

Joey put out the word he was looking for a pro match. They had the freedom to manage their fighter any way they thought best, but they felt it was too risky to tell D'Vito before they were sure they had a victory.

They were contacted by a promoter who offered to put up his fighter, who was a couple of years older than Johnny. Both fighters weighed 155 pounds and would fight as middle weights. Their bout would be three rounds early on in the evening before the main event. The purse was only thirty dollars, but it would still count as a professional fight.

On fight night, a nervous Joey and Dino fussed over Johnny in the locker room as they were getting him ready for his debut.

"Whose dis guy I'm fightin'?"

"I musta tol' you fifty times," said Joey. "His name is Chavez."

"Where's he from?"

"Mexico. Look, Johnny, the kid is older and more experienced than you. He's taller and has a longer reach. Ya gotta be real careful."

"Wadda' ya t'ink Dino? Ya think I kin win?"

"Sure, Johnny," assured Dino as he helped put on the gloves.

Someone opened the locker room door and yelled, "You guys are up!"

As they walked down the isle to the brightly lit ring, Johnny was impressed by the growing crowd and the size of the arena. When they climbed into the ring, Johnny spotted a camera.

"Hey, I'm gonna be on TV."
Some of the spectators near the ring heard his comment and laughed. Even the referee had a grin.
"Those are for the main event, Johnny," said Joey in his ear. "But, they are taping your bout and givin' us a copy."
Johnny realized they were laughing at him and became embarrassed. He felt naked up in front of everyone and wanted to get out of there.
The announcer stepped to the middle of the ring, and a microphone was lowered to him from the ceiling.
"Ladieees an' gentlemen. Welcome to the Plaza Arena tonight for the upcoming heavy weight main event of McMurtrey and Rodriguez. But, now we'll have several preliminary bouts. Our first for the evening will be a middle weight, three round event.
"And now, in the blue corner; from Mexico; weighing in at 155 pounds; in the black trunks; Manuel Chaveeeez!
"And, in the red corner; from Brooklyn, New York; also at 155 pounds; in white trunks; Johnny D'Angeloooo!
"The referee tonight is Tommy Winsloooow."
"Good luck boys!"
The two fighters were instructed by the referee, touched gloves and waited for the bell.
Ding.
The fighters came out of their corners and met in the middle of the ring. They feinted punches a couple of times as they circled. Then Chavez led with a sharp left jab, when suddenly, in a flash, Johnny's right glove shot out under Chavez's extended arm and nailed him on the left side of his face.
To Johnny, it all happened in slow motion. He could see the rounded profile of his glove collapse flat on Chavez's face; the energy of the blow distorting his mouth sending the teeth guard flying; his eyes rolling up into his head; the sweat spray coming off his face and hair; the knees buckling; the body falling into a heap onto the canvass; the referee counting; the crowd leaping to their feet; the announcer declaring a knock out in ten seconds of the first

round. It happened so fast, most observers missed it. Those who were able to see it witnessed an event unlike any ever seen before. The blow was captured on video and was shown on TV sports programs around the country, perhaps the world. The tape had to be slowed down for the blow to be seen.

Joey and Dino were completely stunned. They had never seen Johnny ever show speed like that. As they and Johnny climbed out of the ring, Chavez was still unconscious with a worried looking doctor attending him. Back in the locker room the two men sat on a bench staring wordlessly at their fighter.

"What?" he asked.

"Johnny, how did ya do that?" asked Dino.

"Wadda I do?"

"Ya knocked the guy out in ten seconds."

"Well, I wanted ta get outta dare."

"What?" asked Joey.

"I was embarrassed. Dey was laughin' at me 'cause I t'ought I was gonna be on TV!"

Joey and Dino on the Carpet

The day after the fight, D'Vito had both Joey and Dino on the carpet. From the expression on D'Vito's red face, they didn't think they were going to get any "attaboys".

"Just what da the hell have you guys done??" shouted D'Vito in a cloud of cigar smoke.

Joey spoke first.

"I tho't the kid was ready. He was chomping at da bit, so Wop an' me gave him a chance. Da kid is great!"

"Wit' my money!!" shouted D'Vito.

"He won, didn't he!?" said Dino. "What the hell are you so mad about?"

"Lucky for you guys he won."

There were a few seconds of anxious silence while the two men reflected on that.

"Why'd you guys go around me? What if he lost? What kinda fool would I look like then?"

"Look, Dad," said a fed up Dino. "If we went through you, you probably wouldn't let us do it. If ya did go for it, you'd probably muck it up so bad he'd of lost."

"How dare you talk ta me like that!!"

"You want the truth, don't ya!?"

D'Vito became quiet now and looked down on is desk. Then he raised his head and looked at the two men.

"Joey, we're done talkin'."

The two men got up to leave.

"Dino, you stay here."

Dino sat down again in his chair and Joey left, closing the door behind him.

D'Vito took a long drag on his cigar as he sat behind his expansive desk, looking at Dino. Dino was nervous, wondering what was coming next.

D'Vito was a hard taskmaster and had earlier chastised Dino for debt collection problems. But, he was still willing to work with him because he was good at finding and using talented gang kids. D'Vito decided to let him off the hook, and had him collect only within the family where there were no deadbeats. However, he was still having problems.

"You surprised me, Dino. I didn't think you had the balls to talk ta me the way ya did."

"I-I'm sorry Dad. It just slipped out."

"What's da matter? How come yer all shaky? You been drinkin'?"

"I think I need a break. I haven't been sleepin' too good."

"Why not?"

"I can't get some in our own family to pay up on their loans. And, I'm afraid to tell you, 'cause I know you're gonna run outta patience with me."

"Sounds ta me ya need some help," said D'Vito, as he saw Dino was close to weeping.

"Yeah, maybe I could use a little."

"Hmm," thought D'vito. "Who's da biggest offender? Who owes da most?"

"That would be Lenny."

"How much is Lenny into me for?"

"About five grand."

"Has he ever paid back anything?"

"No. Nothing."

"How come you don't lean on him?"

"He'd eat me for breakfast!" gulped Dino.

"Yeah. I think yer right. We're gonna have a family meeting tomorrow night. I'll bring up da problem there and we can all talk about it. Why don't you knock off da rest of the day an' try ta get some sleep."

"Gee, Dad. Thanks. Thanks a lot."

The Meeting

D'Vito was into several businesses that were controlled by subordinates, who managed by what ever method that would bring in the most money. He would loan money to his managers as needed to do their jobs, but he expected the money back, with interest, according to a strict payback schedule.

The meeting room was upstairs in Joey's gym. The building had long ago been a sheet-metal factory and warehouse, and was now owned by D'Vito. The lower windows had been covered by sheet-metal to keep out prying eyes and intruders. The upper windows allowed some daylight, but not much as they were covered by years of grime. D'Vito liked it that way as it attracted little interest, and there were no snoopy neighbors.

Before the meeting, Dino made copies of the agenda, and set up eight chairs to a rectangular wood veneered meeting table. The table sat in an alcove within a large room. It was set up with three chairs on each side, and one at each end.

D'Vito would rarely attend the meetings in person. Dino would set up the room, distribute the agenda, run the meeting, collect the status reports and bring them to D'Vito the next day.

The managers began to arrive about ten minutes before the meeting was to start. They immediately headed for the bar and made themselves drinks. The room became abuzz with greetings, conversations and laughter. As they began to sit down, Dino stood near the end of the table with copies of the agenda and watched as each selected his chair. The last one to be seated was Lenny, and as always, he took the chair at the open end of the table.

There was a reason for this. That end was considered to be the head of the table and Lenny was a bully. He would push out anyone else who tried to sit there. No one tried to take him on, and he had delusions of succeeding D'Vito someday.

Dino passed out a copy of the agenda. There was only one item, "Collections."

"Hey, Wop, what da hell is dis?" guffawed, Lenny. "You t'ink yer big enough ta make me pay you?"

"It's not my money, Lenny. It's Dad's."

"Well, den you'd better pay it, Stoopid, or he'll beat the shit outta you fer not collectin'." grinned Lenny. Then he added, "I t'ink you gotta bigger problem than me."

The other men at the table were quiet while Lenny was bashing Dino. Then Lenny saw their eyes widen as they saw something behind him. Turning in his chair, he too became wide eyed as he saw D'Vito standing about four feet behind him with a baseball bat in his hand.

"Hello, Dad," they all said, nearly in unison.

"You want my chair, Dad?" said a terrified Lenny, as he jumped up.

"No. You sit down Lenny."

Then D'Vito addressed the group.

"It's come to my attention, dat some of you are behind in yer loan payments. Gentlemen, it's time ta pay up. Now, I know sometimes it's hard ta come up wit' the money, but ya gotta at least make the effort to avoid disciplinary actions. Any of you dat's behind in paying up, I want ya to tell me right now."

A bespectacled man of about fifty stood up.

"Yeah, Dad. I'm behind about five-hundred," said Carlos, who was into commercial real-estate. It was his job to buy into small businesses, and skim off the assets.

"How much did he borrow, Dino?"

"Ten-grand."

"How much more time you need, Carlos?"
"About a week."
"You got it. Who else is behind?"
"I'm behind fifteen-grand," said Antonio.
"How come?"
"Um, an oversight. I kin write a check, right now."
"Do it an' I'll forgive you. Who else?"
Lenny was sweating bullets.
"Uh, I guess I'm a little behind," he said.
"How much does Lenny owe, Dino?"
"Five-grand."
"For dis month?" asked D'Vito.
"Actually, he should have been paying a thousand a month," said Dino.
"He's behind five months?"
"Uh, look Dad, I could pay it back right now if I had my check…"
D'Vito swung the bat, breaking Lenny's right arm. The blow was so hard, it knocked Lenny out of his chair and on to the floor. He cried out in pain and tried to fend off the next strike, exposing his right rib cage.
"No! Don't!" he screamed as the next blow broke two ribs puncturing his lung. He lay on the floor coughing up blood.
"Let dis be a lesson to all of you. Don't get behind in yer payments, unless ya gotta good excuse. *Capisce?*"
Then he addressed Lenny, who was still on the floor.
"I got another job for you, Lenny. Yer gonna take over Dino's collection job, only dis time it's different. Yer gonna make up any shortages outta yer own money. An' God help ya if yer ever short."
Then he threw down the bat and walked out.
Lenny was getting his breath back and glared at Dino.
"Yer gonna pay fer dis, Wop," he spat out with blood dribbling from his chin.
Dino grinned back at him.
"Only my friends call me Wop, an' you ain't my friend."

The Rise of a Fighter

The next morning, Dino was called into D'Vito's office.
"Sit down, Dino," said his boss.
Dino sat in the big black leather chair in front of D'Vito's desk.
"I been doin' some t'inkin' since last night's meetin'. Since Lenny's gonna take yer job of loanin', you got time ta work wit' dat fighter kid, what's his name…?"
"Johnny. Johnny D'Angelo."
"Huh. Another wop. Anyway, I t'ink you should spend all yer time wit' him. Joey says he can make a champ outta him. Help Joey where ya can, but mainly I want ya ta make sure nothing' happens to the kid."
"What do you think might happen, Dad?"
D'Vito lit up a cigar and leaned back in his chair while he thought how to answer Dino's question.
"He could become a target by some other family. You know, jealousy. Be sure ta always carry yer heater," D'Vito warned.
"I always do."
"Good. Another t'ing, don't solicit any press stories. I don't wanna advertise dis kid too much. At least not yet."
"There'll be sports reporters at the fights," cautioned Dino.
"Just don't advertise who he'll fight next, or our intentions. Let dem news bastards figure t'ings out for demselves. An' don't you an' Joey bring dis kid along too fast where he'll attract attention."
"Who's gonna be his sponsor?"

"Let's say he's sponsored by 'Joey's Gym.' Now, I want everyt'ing to be legit. I don't want trouble from da Boxing Commission, or IRS, or anyone else. I don't want anyone to trace t'ings back ta me."

Dino swallowed hard, "Ya know, Dad, this will cost some money. Joey's going to need a new gym, with straight clientele and uncooked books. Me and Johnny should move out of our neighborhood, and…"

"Look, Dino, you ain't tellin' me somet'in' I don't know. You and Joey can have an account wit' all da money you'll need. 'Joey's Gym', will be da front. All business transactions will go t'rough there. Joey'll be da owner an' manager of da gym an' you'll be his partner."

"Wow!"

"One last word, den I don't wanna see you again. Take two years to bring dis kid to da top five. If he can't hack it, ya gotta le' me know right away, so I don't keep spendin' on you guys."

With that, Dino shook D'Vito's hand and left his office.

Dino couldn't believe what just happened. D'Vito actually trusted him enough to give him a blank check. He drove his red Caddy straight over to Joey's gym, where he found Johnny working out with Joey.

"Hey, Champ, Joey, guess what?" Dino called out as he ran over to greet them

Within a few weeks, Dino and Joey found and rented the perfect building for the new gym.

"We gotta get a sign, Joey."

"I can see it now," said Joey. "Joey's Gym!"

"Nah, it should say, 'Joey's Gymnasium'!"

"There ya go. Somethin' high class."

They both laughed, intoxicated by money and the dream of success.

They had much to do.

They transferred some of the equipment from the old gym, and junked the rest. Then they bought a lot of new equipment and furnishings for the new gym. Joey also had a plush office and living quarters in the new building.

Dino and Johnny found and leased a suite for their new home, only a couple of miles from the gym. They had a two car garage, patio, deck and a penthouse with a skylight, where they could throw future parties.

"Man, dis is livin'!" said Johnny as he lounged in the living room, picking up the television remote.

"I'll say," added Dino, as he sat at the dining table reading the daily newspaper.

"Ya know, I don' know who yer boss is, but he must have a lot of money."

"I don't think it's all his money. It must be coming from his corporation."

"What did you say he does, again?"

"Um, he's in the investment business."

"So, his company pays fer all dis?"

"Right."

"So how much am I worth?"

Dino got tired of Johnny's questions and wanted to read the paper.

"Look, Johnny, I have no idea how much you're worth, and I don't think anyone else does. It's kind of like gambling, only in our case, it's more like a sure bet."

Johnny screwed up his face as he thought that over.

"So, what's da bet?"

"That you will be one of the top five rated fighters, in your weight class, within two years."

"Not da top?"

"That's all I'm gonna say about it, Johnny," said Dino as he returned to the newspaper.

Johnny was quiet for a while, then, "Can I ask one more question?"

Dino gave a sigh, "What?"

"What is exactly yer job? I mean besides dishing out money."

Dino knew what he meant, and decided to tell him.

"My main job is to protect the investment."
"I t'ought so," said Johnny, with a smile.

***

Dino and Joey got their gym up and running, and got rid of all the "bums" and "wanabes" that hung out at the old gym. They hired good trainers to work with new clients.

At first, Johnny was matched with lower ranked contenders and gradually crept up the totem. But, he had to be warned several times to not end the fight too early. He complained bitterly to Dino and Joey as they attended to him in the corner.

"Hey man! What's da matter wit' you guys! I can take dis guy out in the next round wit' one punch."

"Easy, Johnny," said Joey.

"Come on, Johnny," said Dino. "Wait until at least the fifth round before ya unload on him."

"Why!"

"Well, there're people here who paid to see you fight. They won't get their money's worth if you end it too soon. And, the sports reporters are here. Ya have to give them something to watch."

Johnny wasn't happy, but he did drag it out to the fifth round when he knocked out his opponent with the first punch. The crowd went wild and enjoyed every minute of the fight.

Joey and Johnny went to the locker room, and Dino stayed at ringside to talk with some of his people who began cleaning up. He was approached by Jimmy Olafson, a sports reporter with the Brooklyn Eagle.

"Hello, Dino."

"Hi, Jimmy. What's goin' on?"

"That's what I was wondering," said Jimmy. "Something don't smell too good."

"Maybe you should change your underwear, Jimmy."

"I think you're holdin' yer fighter back."

"Why would you say a thing like that?"

"'Cause I've seen him fight before. He coulda taken that other kid out in the first round. Besides, he looked peeved after ya talked to him after the first round."

"Is that right?"

"Don't you work for D'Vito?"

"No. Who told you that?"

"You have any enemies?"

"A few. What reason would I have to have my fighter pull his punches?"

"Well, suppose you get your fighter up near the top and then you turn him loose. Then, he wins all his next fights in the first round. That would get a lot of attention, right?"

"I'd say so," said a guarded Dino.

"Now, say your fighter finally gets a fight for the championship. If you were a betting man, what fighter would you bet on?"

"With no losses, and a lot of knockouts in the first round, I'd bet on my fighter."

"So would I. But, suppose your fighter loses. Can you imagine how much money the bettors going with the champ would make?"

"So, you think this is a scam? Wouldn't the owners do better with a champion on their hands?"

"Over how many years? Come on, Dino, I can't believe you bought into that fairy tale."

"So, what are you gonna do, Jimmy?"

"Well, I'm not going to write about it. After all, it's only hearsay. I wouldn't want to be sued for slander."

"Or shot."

"Right."

"I think you heard this from Lenny."

"Who's Lenny? You know, I just can't believe you haven't figured this out."

"If I were you, Jimmy, I'd stay away from Johnny and me."

"See you around, Dino."

Dino watched him disappear through the door and out into the night. Then he walked, slowly, to the locker room, where he found Joey.

"That went over pretty well, don't ya think?" asked Joey.

Dino didn't say anything, but sat down in a chair. Now he knew. Now he understood how this would all play out. Johnny would never become the champion.

Almost a Champion

Time passed. Joey's Gymnasium became a famous place for boxing bouts. Most of the big fights were held in the Civic Arena, which could accommodate large crowds. But Joey's place was big enough for lower ranked matches, which were even televised.

The biggest attraction of Joey's Gymnasium, however, was its famous product, "Killer Johnny D'Angelo." It was his home gym and people hung around just to catch sight of him, or get his autograph.

Everyone knew he'd be the next middleweight champion. Dino had removed all restrictions on him. Over the last three fights he was free to throw his famous quick punch. Two of the last three bouts ended in the first round, and one in the second. Now, he was matched with Pedro Gonzales, the current champion. The title fight would be held in the arena in three days.

"Man, I'm gonna be the champ!" shouted Johnny, as he danced around their living room.

Dino sat on the couch trying to watch the news and sip his bourbon and seven. Then the sports segment came on.

Johnny stopped his celebrating and sat next to Dino.

Announcer:

"And, on Friday night we'll have the match of the decade, right here in Brooklyn. Killer Johnny D'Angelo will challenge Pedro Gonzales for the Middleweight Championship of the World.

In my view, it'll be a walk in the park for D'Angelo. After seeing some of his fights, and that famous lightening quick punch, well, I'd put my money on the Killer."

"Did ya hear dat, Wop? He said he'd bet on me."

"Yeah, yeah I know, Johnny. You keep reminding me all the time how yer gonna take Gonzales apart. Why don't ya give it a rest?"

Johnny was stung by Dino's lack of enthusiasm.

"Hey, what's da matter, Wop? You don't seem interested anymore."

"Look, I gotta headache, an' quit calling me Wop!" said Dino, with some heat.

"Dino, what da hell's da matter? Ya said ya wanted ta get outta yer other job, an' ya did. Now everyt'ing is gravy. I don' know what yer mad about. Did I do somet'ing?"

Dino felt terrible. Already he was hurting Johnny, and this was nothing compared to what he'll do to him in a few days.

"I'm sorry, Johnny. It's this terrible headache. You can call me Wop. We're still tight. I think I'll go ta bed."

"OK, Wop, see ya in the morning."

Dino went to his room and lay down on the bed. The huge apartment was like a villa. He had a king size bed all to himself. Neither he nor Johnny entertained any girls since they moved in. Neither of them had the luxury of time or interest in women because of the regimen they were on.

Now, soon, will be the end. It was like waiting for a huge climatic event that will be the end of the world. He reached into his pocket and pulled out the letter and read it again.

Dear Son,
The family wants you to come down on the 7th.
Love,
Dad

On the day of the fight, Johnny was doing some light workout to loosen up. Dino had to let Joey know about the letter so he wouldn't die of a heart attack during the fight.

"Joey, I heard from Dad."

"How come? I t'ought we wouldn't hear from him... Oh-oh! He wants us ta t'row da fight, right?" said Joey.

"In the seventh round."

Joey was philosophical, "Well, it was fun while it lasted. You tol' the kid yet?"

"Not yet. God, I hate to."

"You t'ink you're hurtin' over dis, it's gonna be terrible fer him. When ya gonna tell him?"

"Just before he goes into the ring."

It was only minutes now, before fight time. Dino, Joey and Johnny were getting ready for their walk to the ring.

"Man, oh man, oh man, am I hyped!" said Johnny as he danced and shadow boxed around the locker room.

Dino and Joey were sitting on a bench, both very nervous. Finally, Dino spoke.

"Johnny, come here. I got something to tell you."

"Yeah, Wop?" he asked as he danced up to Dino.

"You're going to have to do something in the seventh round."

"I get it. Ya want me ta stretch it out ta da seventh ta make a show outta it. Yeah, sure, I kin do that."

"No. That's not what I mean."

"Wadda ya want me ta do?"

"I want you to lose the fight, in the seventh."

Johnny couldn't believe what he had just heard.

"Yer kiddin, right?"

"No."

"Yer crazy, Wop! I ain't gonna do dat! Why would I do dat?"

"Because I'll get killed if ya don't! And so will you and Joey."

"Why do I have to do dis? I'm ranked now! I'm gonna be Worl' Champion!" he begged. "I could be someone! If I do dis thing, I'll never be ranked again!" Then he broke down and cried real tears.

"List'n you punk!" shouted Dino. "We made a fighter outta you. We paid your expenses! Now, you owe us!" Dino was also devastated but had no choice.

When they walked to the ring, the crowd went wild. This was going to be the new champion. He was a hometown boy. Everyone was on their feet, chanting, "Johnny, Johnny, Johnny…,"over and over. But, all he could do was just look straight ahead.

The ring was brightly lit by big overhead flood lights. The ropes were covered in black plastic to protect a body thrown against them, and the clean white canvas would later be splattered with blood.

There were no preliminary bouts to be fought on this night. Only the fifteen round main event. The champion, along with his handlers, was already in the ring, dancing around and shadow boxing. Then Johnny, Dino and Joey climbed in and joined them.

The ring announcer stepped to the microphone, lowered from somewhere up above, and made the introductions. When he announced "Killer Johnny D'Angelo" as a local boy, the crowd went wild, cheering and stamping their feet. All this time, Johnny would only look down at his feet. The handlers got out of the ring and the fight started.

"Jeez," said Joey. "He's not even tryin'. He's gonna get killed."

Now, Dino was worried Johnny might not even make it to the seventh round. That would be bad, as bets are usually made on who wins and in which round.

At the end of the first round, Johnny was already bloodied but still on his feet. The crowd was silenced, probably because they'd all bet Johnny would win by a knockout by this time.

The referee came to Johnny's corner.

"You alright kid? I don't think I even saw you throw a punch."

"I'm OK."

"You'd better start punchin' or I'm gonna stop the fight," said the ref. Then he moved away to get ready for the next round.

Rounds two and three were pretty much like round one, only Johnny was making a little more effort to fight back.

In round four, the champion stood Johnny up with a short right uppercut, and then a hard left punch to the face. The kid went down like a falling slab of wood. The referee started counting and Dino was nearly having a heart attack.

"Get up, Johnny! Get up!" shouted Dino.

He did get up and managed to convince the referee he could continue. Again and again he took blows to the head. A huge mouse puffed up around each eye, causing them to nearly close.

As soon as he was able to find his corner, Joey and Dino were ready for him. Joey took a small penknife from his pocket and Dino blocked the officials' views with a towel. Large amounts of blood spurted out as the blade pierced the swellings around the eyes. Now he could see again.

In the fifth and sixth rounds, Johnny was able to go the distance, and it seemed to Joey and Dino Gonzales was now pulling his punches. He either was in on the plan, or he was trying to stretch out the fight for reasons of his own. The crowd became angry. Originally, they came to see a new champion in the making, but Johnny disappointed them so much, they turned against him and wanted Gonzales to shred him in pieces.

Only seconds into the seventh round, the champion hit Johnny hard along the right side of his head. He went down on his stomach and was out cold. Gonzales was happy and danced around the ring with upraised arms, and the crowd stood and cheered.

Joey and Dino went to Johnny's side and helped the broken fighter to his feet.

Gus

All three men left town. Johnny went to Vegas, and didn't know or care where Dino or Joey ended up. He tried to do a little street business like he did before Dino found him. It was hard. Other people had their areas staked out and weren't too friendly to interlopers. But, he knew how to fight and was not easily intimidated. He ousted one lowlife called, "Peanuts," and took over his area.

Peanuts had a few guys working for him, and now they worked for Johnny. He kept the best ones and chased off the rest. He had his guys doing the usual "thuggery" for him, like shakedowns and burglaries, but he kept his hands clean and lived in a fairly nice apartment.

One morning, while he was sitting at his kitchen table drinking coffee and reading the newspaper, there was a knock at the door. Surprised, but not alarmed he opened the door and there stood a man, about thirty, and nicely dressed.

"Johnny?" he asked with a smile.

"Yeah."

Then the man pointed a gun and pulled the trigger.

Click.

It misfired.

Wham!

Johnny's quick fist didn't. The gunman fell into a heap. He quickly searched his pockets, but there wasn't a thing on him. Not even a comb.

He picked up the gun and pulled the man into his apartment. He thought about killing the guy, but then decided to ask questions instead. The man stirred, and saw his own gun looking back at him.

"Get up," said Johnny as he pulled the man to his feet.

"Please don't shoot me," said the man, as he wobbled.

Johnny directed him to sit on the sofa while he pulled up a chair.

"Who da hell are you?"

"No one you know, or have heard of."

"Why'd ya try ta shoot me?"

"For a thousand bucks."

Even Johnny could tell this was no ordinary hood.

"Someone hired ya ta kill me? Who?"

"I don't know. It's a business. I get an assignment and well, here I am. First time my gun didn't go off."

Johnny was fascinated. He had never met a hired killer before.

"How long you been doin' dis."

"About a year."

The man seemed friendly with no qualms about talking.

"What'd ya do before?"

"I was in the Army."

"Yeah?"

"Special Forces," the man added as he tenderly touched his jaw where he'd been hit.

Johnny was ready for more trouble as he saw the man's eyes were now focused on the gun.

"What's yer name?"

"Gus."

"Don't try nothin', Gus. I'm a lot quicker den ya t'ink."

"So, what are you gonna do, now?" asked the man, as he leaned back on the sofa.

Johnny sort of had a tiger by the tail. If he let Gus go, maybe he'd try again and be luckier. On the other hand, if he killed him, maybe who ever sent him would send someone else.

"Who wants me dead?"

"I dunno."

"Who sent ya?"

Gus shrugged his shoulders.

"How'd ya know how ta find me?"

Gus gave a long sigh

"I get instructions of all I need to know from a messenger."

"A messenger? From who?"

"I dunno. I get the order, I fill it, it gets verified and then I get paid."

"Man, dat sounds like a real business," said Johnny with interest. "Seems like a can o'worms, though. How'd ya keep from gettin' caught?"

Gus shrugs again.

"It's all thought out."

"I wanna talk to yer boss."

"Why?"

"Maybe I could do dis t'ing."

Johnny didn't realize this had been a setup. It was a test and he passed with flying colors.

A New Career

"They" had been watching him since he retired from boxing. "They" knew how he'd react in almost any situation. "They" knew he had instant reflexes and was lightning fast, and that he lived alone in a small city, in a quiet neighborhood, and he kept out of trouble.

On the down side, he knew nothing about guns, even though he was associated with a few criminals. But, these were temporary problems that would be corrected.

Gus became his mentor. He'd be working for "Pacific Coast Tooling, Incorporated," a real firm with real employees. His title was Consulting Engineer, where he would be sent out in the field to service "customers."

His tools were issued by the company; an 8 mm German made Mouser scoped rifle with a hair-trigger, and a small Colt .25 automatic that could be hidden in the palm of a hand.

Everyday he was to fill out a time card for nonexistent project accounts, and mail them to a PO Box. So it looked like a normal business. His "projects" would be sent to him by a messenger, and sometimes by U.S. mail.

Gus showed Johnny how to assemble the rifle.

"Look here, Johnny," said Gus, as he opened the box containing the weapon. "The barrel is detachable, and the stock folds up making it compact and easy to ship or to carry."

"Yeah, I kin see dat."

"All you have to do is to screw the threaded barrel on to the frame, and unfold the stock. It'll click into place," said Gus as he assembled the rifle.

"Purddy nifty," said Johnny as he looked it over. "How come it's got two triggers?"

"Ah, that's one of the special features of the weapon. Now watch. First I cock the rifle with the bolt action (click, click). Then I set the hair trigger mechanism by squeezing the rear trigger (click). Then I barely touch the front trigger (click). If there had been a round in the chamber, then there'd be a hole in your wall."

"Wow! Kin I try it?"

"Sure," said Gus, as he handed him the weapon.

Johnny played with the triggers then asked, "What's dis screw for? Between da triggers?"

"That little screw sets the sensitivity of the hair-trigger. You can set it so a butterfly could fire it."

"Really?"

"Sure."

Johnny looked puzzled.

"Why would ya want somet'in like dat."

"Well, if you barely touch the trigger to fire the rifle, there's less chance of moving off the target."

"Huh. So what's dis fat t'ing on da end of da barrel?"

"A sound and flash suppressor."

"A what?"

"I'll show you when we go to the firing range."

"An' dis t'ing looks like a telescope."

"That's what it is. I'll show you how to use that too, on the range. But, now, I want to show you this little guy," said Gus as he handed the small automatic pistol to Johnny.

"Cute li'l t'ing ain' it."

"Cute and deadly. Nothing to learn about. Just point and shoot, but in close and in the head."

The next day they went to a private firing range. It had been part of an Air Force base that had been closed for a decade. The range had been bought by an exclusive gun club and had to be scheduled for use. Gus reserved the whole range for the day.

"The place is ours, Johnny," said, Gus.

"I kin see dat."

Gus had brought some targets which were concentric circles around a bull's-eye. He attached it to a rope and pulley mechanism, like an old clothesline, and moved the target out to a hundred yards.

"Can you see the bull's-eye, Johnny?"

"Barely."

"Now rest the rifle barrel on the railing so it's steady, and look through the scope."

"Yeah. Now I kin see it."

"Good."

Then Gus removed the suppressor from the barrel, and put five rounds into the magazine.

"Watch, Johnny. I pull back the bolt and a round pops up. I slide the bolt forward and the round get's pushed into the chamber."

"Yeah. I see dat."

"OK. Look through the scope and put the crosshairs on the bull's-eye. Then squeeze the front trigger."

Bang.

The recoil hit his shoulder hard.

"Did you hit it?"

Looking through the scope, Johnny could see a bullet hole in the target.

"I hit da target, but way to da right."

"Try again and keep the butt tight against your shoulder."

Johnny cocked the gun and fired.

Bang!

"Dat's a li'l better but still to da right."

"Okay. Let's adjust the hair-trigger and see what that does."

Gus used a small screwdriver and turned the sensitivity screw. Johnny cocked the rifle and was about to take aim, but it went off when he touched the trigger.

"Whoa!!" he yelped and dropped the weapon.

Another adjustment another try and he hit the mark. After firing a few more rounds, Gus put the suppressor back on the barrel to show its effect.

Ka-chung!

He tried out the pistol with the target close in front of him, just to get used to it.

They spent the day at the range and many more days later. Gus was a good instructor and taught him all he had to know about the business. Soon he would go out on a real assignment with Gus.

First Score

Johnny saw that the business had been well thought out. Every two weeks he'd get a payroll check in the mail. When he begins to really work, the firm would send non-traceable payment for him to an off shore account. He would never see or hear directly from anyone in the Special Services Department, except Gus.

"Say, Gus, I've been wonderin'. Do ya have any idea who yer whackin', an' why?"

"We're not supposed to be wondering. If you learn too much, *you* might get whacked yerself."

"I t'ink a lota hits are fer da big Mafia bosses."

"Probably, but I think this business was started and is run by some astute people. Maybe CIA."

"Really? Why do ya t'ink dat?"

"Because from time to time I've read where some politician, or his aide, ends up as a suicide. The first thing I think is he got whacked."

"Really?"

"We're not the only fish in the tank. There're specialists out there that know how to make a whack job look like a suicide, an accident or even natural causes."

"Dis mus' be a real big outfit."

"Hey, it's time for us to go."

They picked up their equipment bags, and placed them into the trunk of Gus' car, which they swapped for another from a lot a few miles away. Then they began their hour and a half drive. Their quarry lived in an expensive home overlooking the ocean between Los Angeles and San Diego.

"One thing you gotta remember," said Gus, "drive very carefully. You don't want a ticket and give some cop a reason to search the car."

"You ever get a ticket?"

"Not one. But, if it ever happens, remember you've got a wallet with ID in the glove compartment."

When they reached the neighborhood of the target, Gus drove by the home.

"Here's his driveway," said Gus. "It goes on up a half-mile to the top of the cliff."

"Somet'in' mus' be goin' on. Look at all da cars," said Johnny.

"He must be having a party."

Gus continued along the road that soon ended. They then took an old logging road, which climbed and followed the contour of a canyon. Eventually, they came to a stop directly across and a little higher than their intended victim's home.

They got out of the car, assembled their weapons, and walked through a small stand of trees. Now they had a clear view of the north side of the house, some distance away. Both men sighted in their rifles, to determine the range.

"What did you get, Johnny?"

"A little over 700 yards."

"Me too."

"Can we hit sumptin dat far?"

"It's a stretch, but possible. There's no wind."

It was ten o'clock PM, and the air was clear and cold. A full moon lighted the landscape. The music from the party drifted across the canyon, and from their rifle scopes they could watch the people through the windows as they danced, and chatted, and ate, and drank.

"Which guy's da target, Gus? Dere mus' be forty or fifty people."

"It's the big bald guy. He's the one who owns the house."

"What'd da t'ink da party's about?"

"I think it has to do with his daughter. This is her eighteenth birthday."

Johnny pulled away from his scope and looked incredulously at Gus.

"Yer kiddin', ain't ya?"

"No."

Johnny looked again through his scope. Music and laughter drifted in and out with the warm air currents rising up the canyon walls. He could see the birthday girl, laughing and enjoying her family, friends and relatives. He was sure they were Italian because of their mannerisms and the way they were so animated. What he would have given to have had a family like that.

"I can't do dis," said a dejected Johnny.

"You don't have a choice."

"You knew dis girl was gonna have a party. She'll never forget dis."

"I knew he'd be home for his daughter's party. You can't let your feelings get in the way of your job."

"Da only t'ing worse would be ta kill da girl."

"That happens sometimes."

"How could it?"

"Revenge. Someone wants to punish the parents."

"Suppose I didn't do it?"

Gus didn't answer right away, as if to let Johnny know there was an obvious answer.

"You don't have that option, Johnny."

It was Johnny's turn to be silent as he again put his eye to the scope and watched the party.

"This is going to be your shot. I'll back you up in case you miss" said Gus, coolly.

"Should I choot t'rough da window?"

"No. The refraction might cause you to miss."

"Da re-what?"

"Refraction. The glass in the window could cause distortion, which might make you miss."

"Den, what should I do?" asked Johnny somewhat miffed.

"There are some people outside on the patio. Maybe our guy will go out to talk to them. The outside lights should make him an easy target."

The two killers waited and watched. The large bald man seemed the perfect host as he moved through out the house, chatting with guests. Johnny and Gus had already sighted in their rifles for the range the bullet must travel. Then, panning their weapons to the right, they could see something going on in the kitchen. It was the cake. The birthday cake was taken out of a large box and placed on the island countertop. Some of the women were working in the kitchen, and began to put candles on it. The bald guy was herding everyone outside on to the patio. Then the candles were lit and the cake carried out and place on the patio table. The guests and family gathered around the table as the girl prepared to blow out the candles. The bald guy stood on a bench as he proposed a toast to his daughter.

"Now, Johnny! Take your shot now!"

Ka-ching, barked the silenced rifle.

Down went their victim. And then the music, and chatting, and laughter turned into screams.

Old Friends Meet Again

Dino was lying on top of his apartment bed idly watching a rerun of "Cops," when his doorbell rang.
Who the hell can that be? he thought, as he grudgingly got to his feet. When he opened the door, he got the shock of his life.
"Johnny! Hey man, good ta see you!"
"Hi ya, Wop."
"What brings you to Iowa?"
"I gotta new job, an' I gotta see a client in Iowa City. So, I t'ought I'd look you up while I was here."
"How did ya know I was here?"
"Ya know, someone tol' me, but I can't remember who."
"What kind of job do ya have?"
"Here, I'll give ya my card," said Johnny, as he fished in his pocket and pulled one out.
Dino looked at it and was impressed.
"How'd you become an engineer?"
"The company trained me. But, Dino, did you eat dinner yet?"
"No."
"How about we go out and have some Italian food. I'll spring fer it."
"Sure. Then we can get caught up. I know a great place."
They went out the back door of the apartment and under the carport was Dino's red "Caddy" convertible.
"Well, Wop, I see ya still got da "Caddy.""

"I couldn't part with it, Johnny."

"Ya sure kept it nice an' shiny."

They got into the car and Dino drove a couple of miles to a small Italian bistro. They were seated at a table and had their orders taken.

"Man, dis is a little dump, ain't it?" said Johnny.

"But, the food's good," defended Dino. "I suppose with a traveling job like you've got, you eat in the big expensive places."

"Tell me, Wop, what've been doin' since dat awful day?"

Johnny was referring to the day nearly four years earlier when Dino had to tell him to throw the championship fight.

"Johnny, we had no choice. We'd both be dead if you didn't."

"I know dat. Forget about da fight. What are ya doin' now?"

Dino thought for a moment. Was Johnny able to understand how he salvaged himself from the slime of crime, and was trying to become respectable?

"Do you remember when I told you I had been in college and was almost ready to graduate when I ran out of money?"

"Yeah, sure, I remember."

"With the money I made working for D'Vito, I was able to save enough to finish school and continue working on an advance degree."

"So, did ya do dis?"

"Yeah. I went back and finished my last year of college, and now I've just turned in my master's thesis, and I'm starting to work on my doctorate program."

"Oh yeah? What kinda doctor are ya gonna be?"

"I'm studying Psychology."

"Ya mean yer gonna be a shrink?"

"Nothing like that. I'm going to teach."

"So, yer gonna be a professor?"

"Maybe."

Johnny and Dino's conversation change to the topic of working in the D'Vito family. Dino again told the story of D'Vito breaking Lenny's ribs with a baseball bat because he held out on paying back his debts.

"Man, was Lenny pissed off. 'I'm gonna git ya fo' dis, Wop,' he said. I told him, 'Only my friends call me Wop, and you ain't my friend.'"

They both laughed about Lenny getting his comeuppances. Then they both reminisced over the times they had in Joey's Gym. Finally, they finished their stories, paid the bill and left.

Dino parked the car back in the carport and turned off the engine. The two men sat there in the dark, neither seemed to want to get out.

"Johnny, have you heard anything about Joey?"

"No. I haven't heard anyt'ing."

"How 'bout, D'Vito?"

Johnny was quiet a moment and Dino thought he didn't hear him.

"Uh, D'Vito's dead."

"Dead? Did someone whack him?"

Johnny didn't answer.

"Then who's running the family?"

Again, Johnny was slow to answer.

"It's Lenny's family now."

A cold bolt of fear shot through Dino. Johnny's left arm was resting on top of the seatback with his hand lightly touching the back of Dino's neck.

"Tell me again how you found me, Johnny."

He didn't answer.

"You're going to kill me, aren't you?"

"Just close yer eyes an' don't t'ink about it."

"This is really your new job. You're a hit man. This is why you know D'Vito's dead. You killed him."

"Not on my own. I was ordered to."

"By Lenny?"

"By the company. I don' know who places da order wit' da company. It gets passed down ta me an' I do it. Lenny's a good bet 'cause now he's in da catbird seat."

"He said he'd get even with me."

"I'm sorry, Wop. I don' wanna do dis t'ing, but I ain't got no choice. Remember? Dat's what ya tol' me when ya made me t'row da fight."

Dino was close to tears. It was only willpower that staved them off.

"What are you going to do?"

"I've gotta .25 against da base of yer scull."

"Try not to get any blood on the seat covers."

Bang.

The bullet went up through Dino's scull, exited his forehead and smashed into the windshield, then dropped onto the top of the dash. Dino's head and shoulders fell against the steering wheel. Johnny picked up the spent bullet and put it in his coat pocket along with the small automatic. He got out of the car, walked around the apartment building to the street, then halfway down the block and got into a nondescript older car and drove away.

The Company

The Pacific Coast Tooling Company, the employer of Johnny and Gus, had been in business since the end of World War I. It was started as a "job shop" by the wealthy industrialist, Henry Hawkins, by making custom tools for the rapidly growing oil industry. Headquartered in Dallas, Texas, the firm had the unique method of doing business, by fabricating their products out in the oil fields. This gave them an edge over competitors, and allowed them to start up new divisions across the country. Even during the depression years of the thirties, they were one of only a few companies to survive and make money.

Henry Hawkins committed suicide in 1937 and was succeeded as CEO of the company by his son, Henry Hawkins II. The reason for his father's suicide was never discovered. Although no note was ever found, it was obvious that he took his own life, and by a gruesome means. His son was immediately informed, and his first action as the new CEO, was to cover up the suicide and issue a news release that his father died of a heart attack. Cooperative company employees took care of all of the details to support the cover story.

To the grief of stockholders and board of directors, the new company CEO, a young flamboyant man, was somewhat of a daredevil. Henry II, as he liked to be called, was an airplane design engineer as well as an aviator. One of his passions was to design, build and test his own racing planes. He pretty much turned over company operations to senior executives, but he would direct new ventures.

During the Second World War, Pacific Tooling, receive huge contracts from the government to make top secret devices. This laid the ground work for them to take on contracts other than hardware, such as spying and assassinations. Activities bordering on war crimes could be contracted through the company and hidden under the cloak of "top secret".

After the war, the company still provided all sorts of hardware that was used in various endeavors of manufacturing and production. Not only were the products used in the oil industry, but also arms for the militaries of countries the world over. Business was good and profits were in the billions. Henry II became the richest man in the world. No one ever came close to matching such wealth, until some years later, after Henry II was in his grave, Bill Gates and Microsoft came along.

The company still hung on to the clandestine San Diego division of Special Services to fulfill certain CIA contracts. Henry II, realized the profits made by the dark side of the company were enormous and started allowing these services to private business and political organizations. He would never set foot on his own company property, and preferred to do business from some remote location. He spent a lot of time in Las Vegas, and it was rumored he met with some Mafia bosses there and offered services to further their causes. So, for many years the company was at the disposal of anyone, anywhere that could afford their services.

Independent contractors to the company, such as Johnny, became tremendously wealthy. After only six years of service, Johnny was a millionaire. Then something happened.

A contractor was arrested by the FBI for racketeering, and not paying his taxes. His crimes were committed before he joined the Company and somehow he slipped through the screens.

Ring.
"Hello?"
"Johnny, it's Gus."
"Hi, Gus. What's goin' on?"
"I've got to talk to you."
"Yeah? You ain't gonna whack me are you, Gus?"

"Not this time. I've got to talk to you about your job."
"Dis don't sound too good. When can you be here?"
"I'll be there in five minutes."
Gus showed up and told Johnny the news.
"Johnny, we've been cut loose from the company. Apparently someone talked and the company's been called on the carpet by Congress."
"So what's dis all mean, Gus?"
"It means were out of work. The company will disavow any knowledge of this side of the business."
"Wadda dey gonna do, kill us?"
"I dunno, but I think we should get lost."
Johnny, the now retired hit man, decided he would move to Africa.

Into Darkest Africa

When Henry II, the CEO of The Pacific Tooling Company, was summoned to testify before Congress about alleged racketeering activities, any and all information about contractors such as Johnny and Gus were immediately destroyed. The once contender for the world's middle weight boxing championship, and a professional killer was now retired.

He moved to Africa, just in case someone should decide his retirement should be made permanent. He traveled light, only taking a few essentials such as his prized rifle, the .25 automatic pistol, a notebook, some cash and a $15 million line of credit.

His new home was a luxury condo overlooking the Indian Ocean in Stone Town, Zanzibar Island, off the coast of Tanzania. He'd been there before on business trips, but this time it was to find a place of refuge where he could lie low for a while.

He enjoyed the hot sunny days and the white sandy beaches, but he was careful not to become intimate with anyone because he had a fear of diseases. He liked to spend time in bars and after he had a few drinks, he would tell anyone within earshot about his early years in the ring and how he nearly earned the title of Middle Weight Champion of the World. He managed to impress a few people, but some wanted to see some proof he was who he said. He would have liked to have physically obliged them, but he had enough common sense not to be around spilled blood.

When Johnny was not hanging out in the bars, he would spend his time reminiscing. He would sit with a thick, leather bound, zippered, three-ring binder. In it were full-page sized photographs of his work, in chronological order. First were ten pictures of unconscious boxing opponents lying prone on the canvas. The eleventh was of himself after willfully losing to the Champion.

Then there were pictures of forty-two men and five women, who were the victims of Johnny's fifteen years of employment with the Pacific Tooling Company. On the back of each photo was the name of the assassinated, along with where, when, and how the contract was filled.

These were the records of his accomplishments, and he was proud of them. Occasionally, he would sit at a table and pore over each picture and recall the memories of that event. He could never forget his first kill. It was surreal as he and Gus perched on a ridge across a Southern California canyon, waiting for the right second. It was cold enough for them to see their breath, on that beautiful moonlit night, as they watched their quarry through their rifle scopes. It was their victim's daughter's eighteenth birthday party. Johnny remembered the anxiety he felt as Gus urged him to fire. The father of the girl, the gracious host, fell dead before his loving family and friends.

If only he hadn't taken the shot. If he had just refused to do this awful thing, perhaps he could have been spared going down this evil path. But, now it was too late. He could never turn back. He had given his soul to the devil. He would never again feel kindness or love toward anyone.

He continued leafing through the photos until he came to the image of an attractive woman. She was the first of the five women he had killed. She lived in the city of Lake Oswego, Oregon. The young estranged wife of a wealthy Seattle attorney. This was one of the rare times he didn't use the rifle. He simply knocked on the door and when she opened it he shot her with the .25 automatic. Sometime later, he met Gus for lunch and told him about it.

"Ya know, Gus, for a second I was face ta face wit' her. If she was my wife, I couldn't of split wit' her."

"Good lookin', huh?"

"Yeah. She was a beaut. I don't see how a man could do a hit like dat."

Gus smiled at Johnny.

"You were the one who killed her."

"No! He's da one dat killed her!" Johnny protested. "I jus' pulled da trigger."

He continued flipping through the pages until he came to Dino. Dino.

His friends called him "Wop." Dino managed Johnny and helped him to become a world class fighter. Those were the glory days. They were best friends. Dino and Joey, the trainer, had finally brought Johnny to the bout of a lifetime, a tile match with the current champ. He knew he could win. Then Dino gave him the bad news. Johnny had to throw the fight because the family bosses were all betting on the champ. He was never the same. It was then the kernel of anger and hate began to make a black spot in his heart. He hated Dino. A few years later, when Dino's number came up, Johnny felt nothing as he killed him.

After a time, he would lay down the notebook, turn out the lights and lie on his bed. From there he could look out of the window, on to the moonlit sea. To most, it was a beautiful sight to watch the dancing lights of fishing boats, and their reflections on the dark and glossy waters, as the fishers plied their skills to feed their families. Johnny didn't picture it like that. He thought about the fish that died violently on the decks, gasping for breath. He enjoyed watching things die. He was no longer human. He was evil.

One night he took his notebook to his favorite bar, "The Dark Continent", which was in the Ivory Palace Hotel. Most other patrons were European tourists and white residents of Stone Town. The only time Johnny was sociable was when had too much to drink. That's when he liked to talk about himself.

Looking around the room, he noticed three men sitting at a table drinking beer and chatting. Two of the men were about thirty years of age, clean cut, casually attired and were seated adjacent to each other. The third man was older. He had a dark complexion with black hair and beard. He wore hiking shoes, with khaki cargo shorts and tunic. A broad brimmed safari hat was hanging from the back of his chair.

Johnny approached and caught their eye.

"Hi. I'm Johnny. Johnny D'Angelo," he said as he sat at the vacant space at the table.

The barmaid approached with a half tumbler of rye to replace the one Johnny had just drained.

The men were polite and introduced themselves.

"I'm Fred, and this is my brother Eddy, and that's Glen, we've just met."

They all exchanged handshakes, nods and smiles.

"Wadda you guys do fer a living?"

The brothers smiled, hoping someone would ask.

"Eddy, and I are on the faculty of Hunter College in New South Wales."

"Is dat around here?"

"No. We're from Australia."

"Teachers, huh? Wadda ya teach?"

"Well, I have a PhD in mathematics."

"You teach mat'? Wow. You mus' be smart."

Fred laughed.

"What do you do, Johnny?" asked Fred, as the other two men looked on.

"I'm retired."

"From what?"

"I was a fighter, once."

"Really?"

"Yeah. Really. I almos' was Middle Weight Champion of the Worl'."

"What country are you from, Johnny?" asked Eddy. "Your dialect is a little strange to me."

"I'm from da good ol' USA. Brooklyn, New York."

"Ah! That explains it."

The two men exchanged smiles as if enjoying a private joke.

"So, are ya both teachers?"

"Professors," corrected Eddy, a little arrogantly. "I teach linguistics. That's why I was interested in your dialect."

"Is dat right?"

"Yes," said Eddy. "Did you know a properly trained linguist can often determine where a person grew up, sometimes within just a few miles, just by the way he pronounces words?"

"Yeah?"

"Yes."

Johnny turned to Glen, who had quietly been taking in the conversation.

"Wadda you do?"

He smiled and said, "I'm a safari guide."

"Ya mean you lead safaris right here in Zanzibar?"

"No. On the mainland."

"So, Johnny, what is that notebook you have?" asked Fred.

"Dis?" he said as he unzipped the binding. "Dese are some pi'tures. Ya wanna see 'em?" he asked as he slid the notebook to him.

The two brothers leaned toward each other as they turned the leaves over.

"I see the first few are of boxers, what are these others? Famous people?"

"Sorta."

He looked over at Glen.

"When you take someone on a safari, do dey take pi'tures of animals dey kill?"

Glen stubbed out a cigarette butt and looked at Johnny.

"Sometimes."

"Watta ya call dat?"

"You mean trophy pictures?" Glen offered.

"Yeah! Dat's it."

Then to the two teacher brothers, who by now were thumbing through a number of them, "Trophy pitures. Dat's what dey are."

"What? What'd you mean these are trophy pictures?"

When Johnny drank too much, he became a bit of an exhibitionist. At first he was subtle, but then quickly came to the point. He had the feeling of power when he could say or do something that would cause another to recoil in disgust or fear.

"Ya heard what Glen said, didn't ya?"

He was grinning now as he watched the light begin to dawn on the two young men. The brothers had lived most of their lives safely behind the stone walls of academia. They had never met anyone like this before. They could feel an evil chill.

"Y-y-you mean you killed these men?" stammered an ashen Eddy.

"Men? Ya didn't come to da women yet?"

"This is a joke, right?" added Fred.

The sinister grin disappeared from Johnny's face.

"Joke? Nah, yer a joke! You an' yer stupid brother."

The two young men were stunned, and frightened by the outburst.

"Lemme show ya somethin'."

Taking the notebook back, he quickly turned to Dino's picture, the showed it to the men.

"Ya see dis guy? Me an' him were in business together. We was bes' friends. Den one day he tol' me he was goin' back ta college an' be a professor. Like you guys. Now ya see his piture in my notebook."

Fred and Eddy had enough. They quickly got to their feet and left.

Johnny leaned back in his chair and laughed. He could feel the stares from other tables and reveled in it. Then he heard a voice.

"Johnny?"

"What…?"

He turned to his left and there was Glen, calmly gazing at him. He had forgotten about him.

"Yeah?"

"May I see your notebook?"

The Great Hunter

Glen Masters was a forty year old South African, a descendant of the Boers, who came to farm the lush land a century earlier. His ancestry was mostly Dutch with some Portuguese and Watusi resulting in a splendid blending of a man.

As a youth, he worked with a safari leader, who would take wealthy people on hunting expeditions in to the bush. After years of experience, Glen went off on his own. He loved to hunt trophy animals, and found Tanzania, once Tanganyika, to be a rich source for them. The establishing of national parks and sanctuaries were not yet a problem for him as some of the game wardens could be bribed.

Fifty miles off the coast, in the Indian Ocean, was the island of Zanzibar, with its many resorts and tourists. He would at times go there to enjoy fine hotels and restaurants, and keep an eye out for potential prospects. This is what he was doing on the evening he met Johnny D'Angelo.

Glen had taken a room for a few days at the Ivory Palace Hotel in Stone Town. On the first evening he was there, he went into the hotel's bar, The Dark Continent, at a time he knew most of the tables would be taken. He ordered a mug of beer, then looked for an empty chair. He saw two men, obviously tourists, sitting and talking at a table and drinking beer.

He went to them.

"Hello. May I join you?" he asked.

"Please do," said one of the men as they stood up.

"I'm Glen," he said as he extended his hand.

"I' m Fred and this is my brother Eddy," said one of the men. They shook hands and sat down.

"What brings you to Africa?" asked Glen hoping to steer the conversation to his interests, such as hunting.

It was at this time another man came to the table.

It was Johnny.

Glen was disappointed as Johnny brashly took over the conversation. He sat there sipping his beer while he quietly watched as Johnny showed his picture album to the brothers. But, then he slowly became interested. It seemed Johnny was a kind of hunter too and probably had money he was itching to spend. He watched as Johnny insulted and frightened the two brothers away and then threw his head back in laughter.

"Johnny," said Glen.

"What...? Yeah?"

"May I see your notebook?"

He pushed the album down the table.

Glen picked up the notebook, stuffed with photographs. He went through page after page. On the back of each photograph were notations of dates, locations and dollar amounts.

He looked up from the book and at Johnny, who was watching for some reaction.

"Johnny, what is this I'm looking at?"

"Wadda ya t'ink it is?"

"I'd say, none of these people are living right now, isn't that right?"

Johnny sipped his drink and said nothing.

Glen turned over a photo and looked at the writing, and then back at Johnny.

"And, I'd also say, the date of their demise is on the back of each photo. And, I think you must have killed them. Am I right?"

Johnny still remained silent.

"Now, how is it that you would carry such an incriminating thing around with you?"

Johnny shrugged.

"Who's gonna turn me in? You?"

"No, not me," chuckled Glen. "I believe you really did kill these people, and I don't think you'd hesitate to kill me. Tell me. How many people have you killed, all together?"

"Le's see. I t'ink it's forty-two men and five women."

"Forty-two men and five women?" echoed Glen. "That's amazing. Now, why do you carry the notebook around?"

"'Cause I wanna be someone."

"What?" said Glen wide eyed.

"Look, once I had a shot at da Middle Weight Championship of da Worl', an' it was taken away from me. I was dis close," he said with a pinching motion with his forefinger and thumb, "ta having it all. An' den dey made me t'row da fight."

"I wanted ta be someone, an' now I am somebody. I've made millions doin' dis job an' I'm proud of it. I show dese pi'tures to people and dey respect me."

"Maybe it's not respect, Johnny. Maybe it's fear."

"Same t'ing."

Glenn leaned back in his chair and quietly studied his table companion. Looking around the room he could see the nearby tables were now empty. There was no one close by to overhear their conversations.

"Why did you come to Zanzibar?"

"'Cause da company I worked for cut me loose, an' I wanted ta get as far away as I could for my healt'."

"What will you do here?"

"I dunno," said Johnny with a shrug.

"Maybe you should make a new picture album. One you could share with people without scaring them to death."

"Wadda ya mean?"

"You like to hunt, right?"

Johnny took another sip of his drink and leaned back.

"Ya mean people? It was a job, but yeah I liked it."

"But you're retired from that. Why not go on to something new?"

"Like what?"

"Like hunting animals."

"Hunt animals?"

"Not just any animals, but the most dangerous animals in the world. People will respect you. You'll be invited to give talks and lead safaris. You'll be sought out everywhere you go. You'll be on the marquee meeting halls. You'll write and endorse books on hunting."

Johnny was completely swept away.

"Wow! Dats what I want! How can I do dis t'ing?"

"I can help you, Johnny. We can start tomorrow."

"What are dese animals?"

"Well, Johnny, it just happens I've made up a list, and I carry it around for when I meet people like you," said Glen as he pulled out a folded paper from his shirt pocket. He had Johnny's full attention as he spread it out on the table.

"These animals are right here in Tanzania, like the elephant which is the worlds third most dangerous, then the Gorilla, the Cape Buffalo, the Crocodile, the Hippo, the Lion and the Rhino."

"Ya mean da elephant is more dangerous den da lion?"

"Yeah, by comparison the Lion's a scaredy-cat."

"And, da Rhino's not on top?"

"He's dangerous, but almost blind. In the whole continent of Africa the most dangerous wild animal is the Elephant."

Johnny slid the list to him and looked it over.

"Ya say da Elephant is only number t'ree in da wor'l."

"Yes."

"What's number two?"

"The second most dangerous animal in the world is not in Africa. The only places you can find him are in Siberia and North America. He is large, vicious and smart. He's been known to hunt down and kill those who are hunting him."

Johnny hung on to every word spoken by Glen.

"What is it!?" he cried.

"The Grizzly Bear."

"Den what's da worl's most dangerous?"

"You've already bagged that one, Johnny. It's your fellow human being."

Johnny looked at Glen's smiling face and flashing eyes. It was like seeing Dino again, with the promise of adventure and success. Like Dino, Glen had the good looks and self assuredness. The image of what he, Johnny, would like to be some day. The image of self respect.

"How much is dis gonna cost?"

Glen knew he had him snared, but he didn't know what to ask for. He was afraid to suggest an amount where if he asked for too much he'd chase him away or not enough and regret it. He'd have to use his wisdom.

"It depends, Johnny. Do you just want to go out into the bush and shoot an elephant, or do you want to bag all of the animals on the list and be filmed doing it?."

Johnny didn't move a muscle and kept staring at Glen.

"Of course, with the photos," continued Glen, "you can make up advertising posters for your safaris and talks…"

"One mil," Johnny suddenly said.

Glen was stunned and struggled to keep his composure.

"Eh, one mil? One mil, what?"

"One million American dollars."

"Uh," said Glenn, so surprised he hardly knew what to say next.

"An' I want every animal dat's on yer African list wit' movie film, still photos an' an album."

"Right, Johnny," said Glen. "But, to do this means we will have to go where the animals are. Into the national parks."

"Dat doesn't bother me. Give me your bank account number an' I'll transfer da money."

"Uh, Johnny, it would be okay to transfer half the amount now, and the rest…"

"No! I'm gonna transfer da whole amount an' I know you'll give me my money's wort', 'cause if ya don't, I'll add ya to dis album," said Johnny with a straight face, as he put his hand on the notebook.

Glen had a choice. He knew Johnny was a sinister character and dangerous, and now was the last chance to decide to save his life. He was like the fly that buzzed around a spider web and then got caught.

A few days later he checked the amount in his bank account, almost hoping the money wasn't there and it was all a big farce.

But it was there.

A million dollars.

Out of Africa

Time passes. Johnny did manage to kill all of the animals on the Tanzanian list, and was filmed making the kills by three native photographers that worked for Glen. They put together a new album for Johnny, showing his bravery as he shot down animals.

It appeared as if he were incredibly lucky to escape injury or death from charging elephant and clawing lion, but in reality it was the skill of photo editors. Movie documentaries were made rivaling the "Buck Jones" film series of years ago. Johnny was in his glory.

Things were not so well with Glen. He hated Johnny and wished he'd never laid eyes on him. He was afraid of him. Johnny seemed so cold and heartless. They argued constantly. The country had been entangled in a civil war, and the few people looking for poachers were bribed by Glen. As the unrest began to settle down, it was only a matter of time when they would be hunted by the authorities.

"Look, Johnny, we have to end this thing. One of these days we're going to get caught, and it won't be for just poaching."

Johnny looked at Glen derisively.

"I ain't ready ta quit dis gig. What's da matter? Didn't I pay ya enough?"

Glen was in over his head. He had to worry about hiring porters and photographers, disposing of the animal carcasses, game wardens, rebels and soldiers, but mostly he worried about Johnny's vicious moods. It wasn't worth the money he was bought for. Somehow, things got turned around. He was going to snare Johnny and control him, but accepting the huge amount of money put Johnny into the driver's seat. Glen, of course, didn't know it, but his life paralleled that of Dino's, another of Johnny's mentors of the past.

Sadly, things came to an end for Glen during a lion hunt. A big male lion was hiding in the grass only about twenty yards in front of the hunters. A movie camera was rolling and a still camera was at the ready. Johnny was in a kneeling position and had his rifle on target.

Suddenly the animal charged. Johnny could see the lion's eyes were locked on Glen, who did not have his rifle ready.

"Shoot, Johnny, shoot!" Glen shouted.

But, Johnny didn't shoot. He only watched the enraged cat run headlong into Glen's chest, sinking its teeth into his neck and right shoulder. Some of the porters ran. Backup shooters began firing, nearly hitting each other. Flying bullets kicked up the sand around the cat, all of them missing.

"Keep da camera rollin'!" shouted Johnny.

It was over in seconds. The animal dropped the body and ran toward the bush. It was then Johnny fired and killed it. Too late.

He walked over to where Glen was lying. The others in the party had scattered. Glen was fatally wounded and bleeding badly. He opened his mouth, trying to say something, but it couldn't come out. His once bright eyes were open wide, but growing dim. And then, he breathed his last. Johnny added the movie film and still shots of the lion killing Glen to his trophy collection.

Glen had been a prophet when he said Johnny would become a sought after hunter. He had advertised himself as a guide and safari leader in hunting magazines around the world. He would take rich old men out into the jungle, dressed like Glen had been when they first met, with cargo shorts, hunting tunic, wide brimmed safari hat, and polished black boots that went half way up the calf of his leg.

But, he wasn't like Glen at all. He had no feelings. No emotions. He was standoffish and unfriendly. He had to hire a staff to manage the hunts and to speak for him, because he was embarrassed by his lack of education and his accent.

The stabilizing of the government put an end to the bribing of game wardens. Johnny's safari operations came to an end and he fled the country. It was now the right time for him to hunt the second most dangerous animal in the world.

Trent Owen

The Smell of Success

"Look, Phil, you know I love my work, but I can't go on like this much longer. I think it's going to ruin my marriage."

"Hey, you're not thinking of quitting, are you? You're the guy with the energy and vision. If it weren't for you and Anne, we wouldn't be in this terrible condition of success."

Trent Owen worked for a home building franchise company. After a three year stint with the army during World War Two, he used his G.I. Bill entitlement to attend college, and graduated from the University of Washington's School Of Architecture. It was there he met Anne, a beautiful blonde girl, and like him, adventurous. They were married a year after graduation. Then, both of them, joined Carter Homes International, a Seattle firm that designed kitted houses.

Trent laughed.

"I guess that's a pat on the back."

They both laughed at the thought of how small the firm was when Trent and Anne came on board. Now, only five years later, they are trying to manage a multimillion dollar company.

Having a degree in both architecture and engineering, Trent was put in charge of the Design and Manufacturing departments. The company could have all of the parts and modules of a new house delivered to any location in the United States and Canada. The buyers had the choice of assembling the building themselves, or by the company. Most customers preferred to have the house assembled and raised on their own property by a Carter Homes team, causing Trent to constantly travel from site to site to make design changes and solve problems.

Anne worked in the Sales Department of the Seattle home office. The more successful she was at her job, the more it caused them to be separated. Trent decided to have a talk with Phil Carter, the CEO and his friend.

"Tell you what, Trent. I'm going to bring up some ideas to kick around at the next board meeting that might help us."

It wasn't long before Phil called both Trent and Anne to his office. After some chit-chat Phil quickly got to the point.

"Trent, Anne, I brought up the subject of our problem to last night's board meeting, and as a result, I have some good news and some bad news."

The smirk on the Chief Executive Officer's face betrayed the "bad news" as not being too bad.

"Let's hear the bad news first," said Trent.

"Okay. Anne you're fired."

"What? But, I love my job," she quickly responded.

"Hmm. Okay, you're rehired, but to a different job. You and Trent will work together."

Both Trent and Anne were speechless.

"I'm sorry, but that's the board's recommendation. They just couldn't see jeopardizing, in any way, the marriage of our new Vice President of Operations."

"What?" said a shaken Trent, who now had to sit down.

"That's not all. Both of you are going to start taking flying lessons."

"Flying lessons?" said Anne, who also had to sit down.

"Here's the deal. Businesses today have to become more flexible or their competition will eat them alive. Trent, you need to stay out in the field and keep up with the problems and customer suggestions."

Phil's eyes darted back and forth between their faces as he spoke.

"Anne, you can now put your engineering training to work too."

"But, I like sales," she complained.

"You can still work in sales by refining improvements and adding them to our offerings."

With that, she sat back in her chair and listened.

"Phil, you're going too fast," said Trent. "What's this about taking flying lessons?"

"We're going to buy a company plane, in about a year. I want you and Anne to fly to your customers to service them. This will be more flexible than using commercial aviation and ground transportation."

"How long will flight training last?"

"That depends on you. It'll probably take a year."

"How will we have time for lessons?"

Cut your schedules back. We're temporarily hiring a pilot with a plane for you and Anne to get used to the change."

The meeting went on for a while longer, but neither Trent nor Anne could follow because they couldn't take in anymore. Right after they left Phil's office, Trent suddenly stopped.

"I forgot to ask him when my job of Vice President starts."

"I don't think you have to," said Anne as she pointed to a nearby door, with a newly installed nameplate.

Trent Owen, Vice President Operations

Flying Lessons

Leonard Johnson was working at his job as line-boy for Tacoma Flying Service, when he noticed a new Cadillac pull up into the parking lot. A couple in their mid to late twenty's got out and took in a sea of tied down airplanes. Then they noticed Leonard watching them, and they began to walk toward him.

He was standing on a stepladder with a fuel hose draped over his shoulder, pouring gas into the wing tank of a Cessna 170. They stood watching him and he acknowledged them with a nod and a smile. When he finished, he rolled up the hose, got into the plane, started the engine and taxied to an open tie-down space. After securing the plane, he walked back to where they were standing.

"Hi. Can I help you?" He asked.

She was a beautiful blonde lady, and she smiled at him.

"How old are you?" she asked.

"I'm seventeen."

He was surprised by the question and could feel his face become warm.

"Come on, Anne. You're embarrassing the poor guy," said the man.

"I'm sorry," said Anne." It's just that you seem so young to be driving a plane around like that."

"Ah, actually I have a pilot's license," he said, now feeling a bit proud.

"You do?"

"Yeah, and I'm working on my commercial license."

"My goodness," she said." What are all these airplanes parked all over here?"

"Most of them are owned by people who can't afford to fly them, so they just tie them down."

"No kidding. We're Trent and Anne Owen," said the man as he reached out to shake his hand.

"I'm Leonard."

They were very friendly, and they hit it off right away.

"So, Leonard," said Trent, "we'd like to take flying lessons. Who do we see?"

"Oh. Well, follow me."

He led them into the flying school office and caught the attention of Chuck, the manager, who quickly got up from his desk.

"Chuck, this is Trent and Anne Owen."

"Hello," he greeted with a warm smile and a handshake.

"I've got to get back to work," said Leonard as he backed toward the door.

Their instructor would be Everett, who was the school's chief pilot. They flew on an accelerated schedule and seemed to be always in the air, or hanger flying with other students in the pilot's lounge, especially if the weather was bad.

It was on one of those days when the wind was a little too brisk for Trent, who was scheduled for a solo flight. Things weren't too busy so Leonard decided to practice a few landings and take-offs in one of the more advanced trainers, a PT-26, a type used during the war.

"Trent, would you like to come along?" asked Leonard.

"Sure," he said, eager to fly in a different kind of plane.

The cockpit was in tandem, and they were enclosed under a Plexiglas canopy that could be slid open or closed. They taxied to the end of the landing strip, checked out the engine and then accelerated down the runway.

The plane was heavy and underpowered but flyable. They left the airport area and flew over the City of Tacoma. Then they could see a thunderstorm coming in from the west. Leonard went directly back to the airport and started his approach in the same direction he had taken off, only to discover the wind had changed directions. They were coming in downwind and with a ground speed too fast to land. Leonard pushed the throttle forward to abort his landing.

They nearly crashed, and barely maintained control. The plane was so underpowered it couldn't gain altitude. They dodged roof top TV antennas for a mile before he could climb. Leonard looked back at the airport and watched it disappear in a cloud of rain, hail and lightning. He could also see Trent in the rear cockpit and his face was as white as a sheet. Trent later said the same about him.

Leonard found a calm patch of sky about five miles to the southeast and stayed there until the storm moved away from the airport, then, he returned and landed without trouble. When they walked into the pilot's lounge, no one there said a word, but from the looks on their faces they didn't have to.

Then Trent said for all to hear.

"You know, Leonard, I think you just gave me the best lesson, ever. You just taught me to hold my breath for twenty minutes."

Then everyone laughed.

Trent and Anne weren't deterred by the incident, and soon had their private pilot's license. Anne decided to quit at this point, but Trent went on to earn his commercial and instrument ratings. Later, he would drop in to show off his company Beechcraft Bonanza.

Tragedy

True to his word, Phil Carter authorized the purchase of a Beechcraft Bonanza. It was one of the first post war airplanes to be suited for both business and pleasure. The price tag was about $25,000, which was a lot of money at the time. It was a welcomed, new and innovative business tool and a big improvement over the clunky gas guzzling DC-3s or C-46s a lot of firms were using.

He and Anne would fly to cities in the U. S. and Canada to help franchise owners with new house designs that were put out from the home office. Life was good and so was the money. Anne then left the company when she became pregnant.

Trent enjoyed flying so much he continued taking lessons, and earned his float plane rating. They had two children, Peter the oldest, and Suzie a year younger. Trent bought a Cessna 185 on floats, just for the family. It was a wonderful plane. Its 300 horsepower engine allowed them to go into the smallest of lakes for great fishing. They took all kinds of fun trips up to Canada and the south part of Alaska, where they would go into the most remote areas, and see unspoiled nature.

When Peter became a teenager and joined the Boy Scouts, his first campout with his troop was a weekend to Sucia Island on Puget Sound. Suzie was spending the weekend with friends, so Trent and Anne thought it would be fun to fly the Cessna up to the island, and surprise him. They took off from their home on Lake Washington, and headed northwest. They were over the San Juan archipelago in about forty-five minutes. Trent made his landing approach toward Sucia, the most northern of the islands.

He landed the Cessna about five hundred yards off shore, and taxied slowly toward the beach. He was looking out for "deadhead" logs and submerged rocks that could damage the plane. The scouts came running down to the beach, to watch the plane come in, and Trent and Anne could see Peter waving at them. Usually, he would shut down the engine when approaching a beach and Anne would climb out onto the right pontoon to attach a line to the wing. This time the plane was being pushed sideways by the current, and he had to keep the engine running to control the drifting. Anne unbelted herself, opened the passenger door, and stepped out, as she had done on so many other occasions. Trent was still concentrating on looking forward, and to the left for a clear area to beach the plane. Anne attached a line to a tie down cleat under the right wing, and then walked forward on the pontoon, right into the propeller.

Trent heard the prop hit something. He turned to see the empty seat beside him, and instantly knew what had happened. His world suddenly ended. The scouts, including Peter, saw it all. Anne was struck in the head, and fell into the water. Peter dropped to the ground screaming. A scout leader went to his knees, and put his arms around the boy. Trent shut down the engine, too late of course, and went into a state of shock.

A park ranger was also on the beach and witnessed the accident. He and some of the older scouts grabbed the attached line and pulled the Cessna on to the beach. Someone took hold of Anne's body and brought it on to shore. Trent was crying and immobile. They lifted him out of the plane and laid him on the ground. Someone covered him with a sleeping bag. The ranger called his office for help on his radio.

Pain

The following days became a blur to Trent. A friend went up to the island, picked up the plane, and flew it back to the Owen's home on Lake Washington. Trent was in a terrible depression. He blamed himself for the accident. He should have realized Anne would try to do her job of securing the plane. He never told her to wait until he shut the engine down.

Phil Carter, Trent's boss and good friend, tried to reach out to him. He and his wife, Susan, dropped in on him unannounced. They found him inconsolable. They sat in Trent's living-room, and tiptoed around any reference to the accident.

"Do you have any idea when you might be back to work?" asked Phil hoping to see a flicker of interest.

Trent said nothing and looked down at the floor.

"It's been three months, Trent, and we need you back," said Phil, pleadingly.

With teary eyes, Trent looked at his friend.

"Phil, I need more time."

"Okay, Trent. Take as much time as you need."

"I don't want you to carry me, Phil. Let me go. I don't think I'll ever be able to work again."

Susan went to him, with tears running down her face, and patted the back of his hand.

"Sure you will, Trent. You just need a little more time."

Then, with breaking hearts, they left and let him return to his solitude.

A few years later, Peter and Suzie enrolled at the University of Washington, and lived in the student dorms. Phil reluctantly hired someone to permanently replace Trent. He lost interest in almost everything, and never went back to work, and he never flew the Cessna again.

His once sky-toy, sat forlornly on the end of the family dock. If it had been left floating on the lake, the pontoons would have gradually been filled by seeping water, eventually causing the plane to sink. Friends prevented this from happening by having a floating crane hoist it onto the dock.

There it sat, like an ignored family pet that kept begging to be loved. It seemed to speak to him.

Fly me. Please fly me.

He hated the plane and wished it could be sunk in the deepest part of the lake.

It wasn't my fault, said the plane.

"I know! I know! It's my fault!" he shouted. He then broke into uncontrollable sobs and tears.

"The pain! The pain! Will it ever stop?" he cried out from the very depths of his soul.

No. It wasn't your fault.

"I suppose you think it was Anne's fault?"

No.

"Was it Peter's fault? If he hadn't been on that outing with the scouts, we never would have made that terrible flight. Anne would be beside me right now. We would all be happy."

You know it wasn't Peter's fault. Or the Boy Scouts' fault. Or, anyone's or, anything's fault.

One would think Trent's depression had deepened to the point of madness. He was holding a conversation with his airplane, the instrument of his beloved and beautiful wife's death. His trophy. But, the opposite was true. He was beginning to heal. He had allowed himself to venture into those places he avoided for three years.

"But, it has to be someone's fault. Doesn't it?"

No. Things happen that defy reason. People used to call them accidents. You don't hear much about blameless accidents anymore. Everyone wants to find and punish the person responsible. Or, people are even willing to accept blame, and punish themselves for the rest of their lives.

Gradually, Trent's life was beginning to return. He felt as though he were being aroused from a deep sleep, filled with nightmares. He began to notice the sun when it emerged from behind a cloud, and he could feel its warmth. The accident seemed to be slipping into the past. It was still there, and always would be there, on his mind.

He felt like he had emerged from a deep, dark, cold, pool of water, and he was on the surface. He now knew he would survive. What he didn't know was how close he came to drowning in his despair.

He needed to do something. He began to take stock of himself to see what he had left. He had enough money to see his kids through college, so that was not a worry. He wanted to fly again, just not the Cessna. He had read some accounts written by an Alaskan bush pilot, and thought he'd like to do that.

Airplane

One Saturday morning, Trent had Peter drive him to the airport where he had learned to fly. Chuck was surprised to see him.
"Hi, Chuck," greeted Trent.
"Trent! What a surprise."
"This is my son, Pete."
"I'm pleased to meet you, Pete."
"Likewise," responded Peter with a smile.
"Chuck, do you remember the first day I came here?"
"I'll never forget it. You and Anne."
Suddenly Chuck cringed when he realized he'd slipped up and made reference to Trent's wife.
"I'm sorry," he said quickly.
"It's okay," Trent responded.
"I can't tell you how sad we were when we first heard about the accident."
"Thanks, Chuck. I'm trying to put my life back together again, and maybe you can help."
"What can I do?" he asked.
"I'm thinking about moving to Alaska, and I was wondering what would be the best plane to use up there?"
Chuck scratched his head.
"To do what?"
"To fly among the mountains. Maybe into some lakes."
"Are you thinking about becoming a bush pilot?"

"I read some accounts of these guys."
Chuck thought some more.
"I think you now own the plane best suited for that work."
"Really? I was thinking of buying something else."
"Why?"
"Because of the accident."
"Forgive me for saying this, Trent, but a plane is just a tool. Especially, when you'll be using it as a bush pilot."
"Yeah, I know."
"I'll give you my best shot, then you do what you want."
"Fair enough."
"The Cessna 185 is the plane of choice for flying in Alaska. Properly rigged, it'll do nearly anything you ask of it. I think you should have your plane hauled over here and let us go over the whole thing. We'll check it out for corrosion and any other damage, and make sure it's current to all of the structural revisions from the manufacturer. We'll install a new engine and constant speed prop, and amphibian floats."
"Amphibian floats?"
"Yeah. They're pontoons with retractable landing gear. Then you're good for land and water."
"So you think I should use the Cessna?"
"I would."
"How would I get it over here?"
"We'll take care of it."
"How much time will all this take?"
"As long as we don't run into some bad problem, it'll take about a month."
Trent was quiet, while he thought about it, and then decided.
"Okay then. Let's do it."
"We'll get right on it. But there is one thing more."
"What's that?"
"When we finish the plane, we'll have to go to work on you. You're going to need a bunch more training."

More Flight Training

"Okay, Trent," said Everett, straining his voice to be heard over the noise of the engine. "I want you to fly right up this canyon."

It was a beautiful, hot summer day, and they were flying between a couple of ridges of the Cascade Mountain Range. They were at 8,000 feet, but the altitude and temperature didn't seem to have much negative performance effect on the engine or wings.

He obediently navigated the plane right up the center of the canyon, and watched as the stone walls came closer and closer together.

"Everett, there is an exit to this canyon, right?"

"I don't know. I've never been up this one."

"What? How the hell are we gonna get out of this? The walls are too high for us to climb over."

"Why did you fly into it?"

"You told me to," said Trent with anxiety.

"Suppose you're flying some trapper in Alaska and he wants to show you his cabin, and it's in a blind canyon like this one. Are you just going to go into it?"

Trent got the message right away.

"How are we going to get out of this?" he asked, as he watched the canyon walls squeezing together.

"Let me have the plane."

Everett took over the controls and opened the throttle wide. Then he pulled back on the control wheel until the wing nearly stalled. The airspeed dropped off, and he was able to put the plane into a tight 180 degree turn to the left, and head back out of the canyon.

"Here, you can have it back. Your first mistake was to fly up the center instead of off to one side."

A wiser Trent took over the controls. He knew he'd never be caught like that again.

Everett was a wonderful instructor and showed Trent all of the tricks about flying in hostile environments, such as uneven terrain and using short runways. Gradually, the man and machine became as one.

Another hazard to Alaskan flight was the weather. He would use his instrument rating to cope with it.

Finally, he was ready for the flight north. He had sold off everything no longer of use to him, such as the house, and the car. What he didn't sell, he gave to his family and friends.

Everyone came to the airport to see him off.

"I wish I were going with you, Trent," said Chuck. "I think you're going to have a great adventure."

"Remember, don't fly too high or too fast," joked Everett.

He hugged his now grown son and daughter.

"Goodbye, Pop," said Peter.

"Good bye, Daddy," said Suzie.

The tears were flowing as he climbed into the cabin of the plane. He started the engine and gave a final wave. Then he taxied to the end of the runway.

Everyone watched as sun reflected off of the shiny wings and fuselage of the Cessna that now had a name.

Brightly painted in red, on the cowling was its new name.

"Anne."

North

The range of a Cessna 185 with floats is about five hundred miles. Trent made a refueling stop at Prince Rupert, British Colombia, and a layover at Whitehorse, Yukon Territory.

He had something to eat at a restaurant operated by a Chinese family. In fact, he was surprised to see so many Chinese people on the city streets. Then he recalled hearing something about the influx of Asians during the gold rush days, so he was probably seeing their descendents.

He retired to his hotel room and had trouble sleeping. Not because of the excitement of a new adventure, but because of a ruckus taking place under his window. The summer days in the Yukon were long and hot, and Trent had to keep his window open to get some air. His room was on the back side of the hotel. In the alley below, were a group of drunken Inuits that decided to hold a loud party.

As he lay on his bed, he tried to figure how many were there. By counting the different voices he decided there must be at least five men and two women.

He listened and tried to understand what they were talking about. Most of the words were slurred and undistinguishable, but occasionally he got the drift. It was like the old telephone party line, and they were discussing their views of the local news, all at once. Finally, they went home about four o'clock AM and he fell asleep. This was only the prelude to encountering a world he never knew existed.

The next morning, he was up by eight o'clock, had eggs and bacon in the Chinese owned restaurant, paid his bills and was off to Anchorage. The weather was perfect as he wound his way through the high passes. The mountains were similar to the one's at home, but higher and more of them.

As he neared Anchorage, he reported in to the flight control station.

"Anchorage Flight Control Center, this is Cessna 2446 Juliet."

"Go ahead, 46 Juliet."

"I'm ten miles east of your station on a flight plan from Whitehorse to Merrill Field."

"Roger, we'll close your plan. Have a good day."

Trent made his approach, landed and taxied up to the gas-pump.

"Hi, can I tie down here?" he asked a young man who came up to service the plane.

"Sure. Leave your key and I'll gas it up for you."

Trent walked into the FBO (Fixed Base Operator) office.

"Can I help you?" asked a slightly balding, middle-aged man with glasses, from behind the counter.

"Your line-boy is gassing my plane now, and then I'd like to have it tied down."

"For how long?"

"Maybe forever."

The man blinked.

"You want a permanent tie down?"

"Yeah. How much is that?"

"$100 a month, in advance."

"Okay. Is there a car rental around here?"

"We've got a clunker you can use for ten dollars a day," said the man. "Where're you from?"

"Seattle, but I'm moving here."

The man became more curious.

"What will you do here?"

"I want to be a bush pilot."

"Really?" said the man. "Have you ever done anything like that?"

"I've read about it."

The man studied him briefly.

"Well, welcome," said the man as he reached out his hand. "I'm Clayton Scott, but everyone calls me Scotty."

He took his hand with a smile, "Trent Owen."

Right away Trent liked this friendly man because of his sincere greeting.

The line-boy entered the office with Trent's keys, and a clipboard with the fuel sales slip.

"Todd, bring up the Chevy for Mr. Owen," said Scotty, as he took the receipt.

Todd took a set of keys hanging on the wall behind the counter and then went back out the door.

"How do you want to do this? You want me to bill you for everything monthly?"

"Sure, that'll be fine. Tell me, are you a bush pilot?"

Scotty looked down for a moment and then looked back up at Trent.

"No. I used to be, but I've had my fill of it. I'm satisfied by running this business. By the way, we don't use the term, 'bush pilot' much. Sounds too hokey."

"What term do you use then?"

"Some call themselves, contract pilots, or charter pilots, or cargo flyers."

"I'm disappointed," said Trent. "I told all my friends I was going to be a bush pilot."

"Okay, be a bush pilot then," said Scotty with a grin.

"Are there others here? I mean that keep their planes on the field?"

Scotty cleared his throat and hesitated.

"There's something I have to tell you," said Scotty with a serious edge.

"What?"

"One of the pilots has set up a kind of union."

"Union?"

"Well, he calls it that. I'd call it something else."

"What's he do?"

"He threatens other pilots if they don't let him get first dibs on a contract."

"Threaten how?"

"Some pilots have lost planes to fires or other damage. Most of these guys are operating on a shoestring, and can't afford to protect themselves with insurance."

"This have anything to do with you changing jobs?"

Todd drove up in an old Chevy and came into the office.

"Thanks Todd," said Scotty. "This is Trent Owen, Todd. He's going to keep his plane here permanently. So now you'll have one more to take care of."

"Nice meeting you, Mr. Owen."

"Please call me Trent."

"That's a nice plane you've got, Trent. What do you use it for?"

"Bush flying."

Confrontation

Trent drove only a few blocks down the road from Scotty's, and pulled into an inn called, "Ben's Sky Harbor." As he walked through the lobby, he noticed there was also a restaurant and a cocktail lounge. The young woman at the desk greeted him with a smile.
"Can I help you, sir?"
"Yes. I'd like a room."
"Okay. How long would you like to stay?"
Trent thought a minute.
"Until I can find a house."
The woman smiled at him.
"I think we can fix you up. Sounds like you're planning on staying in Anchorage a while."
She handed him a clipboard with a registration form to fill out. When he came to the line asking about his occupation, he paused a moment and then wrote, *Self-employed.*
He handed the clipboard back, and the young woman looked it over, and then looked up at Trent.
"You're self-employed? I assumed you were employed by some company. What do you do?"
"Well, starting tomorrow I'll be a bush pilot."
"Then you don't even have a job? I'm sorry, Mr. Owen, but I can't let you have a room if you don't have anyway to pay for it."
Trent nodded in agreement.
"How much is it for a room?"

"Well, the room I was going to put you in is twenty-five dollars a day."

He produced his wallet and took out three one hundred dollar bills, and handed them to her.

"How about if we start with this, and wait to we see if we'll need more?"

The surprised clerk exchanged a key for the money.

He was tired and went straight to his room and lay down on the bed.

When he next opened his eyes, it was eight o'clock in the evening. Having had nothing to eat since breakfast at Whitehorse, he was famished. He washed his face, combed his hair and then went to the dining room.

"Good evening, sir," greeted the receptionist. "Do you have a reservation?"

"No, I don't." responded Trent.

"I'm sorry, but we're full right now. Are you alone?"

"Yes."

"Would you mind taking your meal in the bar? We serve a full meal there."

"Sure. That's no problem."

"Go on in and find a table," said the receptionist as she handed him a menu.

Trent walked into the darkened room slowly, allowing his eyes to adjust.

"There he is now," said someone faintly.

Trent pinpointed the voice coming from a table where three men sat drinking, across the room.

He walked toward the table and caught the eye of one of the men who stood up and beckoned to him.

"Hi, friend. Would you care to join us?"

"Sure, Trent Owen," he introduced himself. "I hope you don't mind if I order a dinner," he added as he sat down. "I haven't eaten all day."

"No, I don't mind at all, since I own the place," said one of the men with a grin as he returned to his seat.

"I'm Ben Barret, and these two guys are friends of mine, Bob Cannon, and Rick Manus."

The men were cordial and shook hands with Trent.

Through the dim light in the lounge, it was difficult for Trent to see the men clearly. Ben was a husky looking guy, about fifty, and had a broad grin. He was losing his hair, and what he had was grey. His assertive behavior overrode what charm he might have had. His two friends were probably in their forties and seem to be his loyal subjects.

"We were just about to order dinner ourselves," said Ben, as he motioned to a waitress.

"Pick what you want. It'll be on the house."

"Oh no. Please. I'd rather pay for it."

"I insist," said Ben. "You won't get another offer from me."

The waitress was now at his elbow.

"Okay. In that case, I'll take the rib steak, medium-well," he ordered, as he handed back his menu.

"Anything to drink?"

"Just water, please."

"We'll have the usual, Jan, and another round of drinks."

Jan left with the orders and now Trent felt as though he was now the center of attention.

"So, I heard you just flew in this morning, and you're planning on staying here," said Ben.

"That's my plan."

"What kind of work are you in?"

"I'll be flying."

"That's a pretty nice 185 you've got."

"You've seen it?"

"Yeah. Sure would be too bad if something happened to it."

Trent quickly realized he was talking to an extortionist. He could feel Ben's eyes staring at him, looking for a chink or a weakness. He took his time about responding to him.

"What could possibly happen to it?"

The other two men were quietly nursing their drinks and said nothing.

"Fire is one of the biggest problems," Ben replied. "Ain't that right, guys?"

The other two men nodded and answered in the affirmative, like puppets.

"Do you mean to say planes around here just burst into flame for no reason?"

"Yeah."

"While they're flying?"

"Oh no. While they're on the ground."

"What could cause a thing like that to happen?"

"There's a theory that because of the long summer days, the angle of the sun is unusual and somehow causes spontaneous combustion."

Trent could smell trouble, and he was never one to run away from it. He wanted to probe as much as he could without setting off any defensive alarms in Ben's mind.

"Are you a flier, Ben?"

"Almost everyone's a flier up here. I'm a contract pilot and I've been one for years."

"How about you guy's?" Trent asked Bob and Rick.

"They're pilots who work for me."

"Bob," asked Trent, "have you ever seen this thing happen? I mean parked airplanes catching on fire?"

Bob was nervous and looked at Ben as if asking permission to speak.

"Tell him what you saw, Bob."

"Uh…yeah. I remember about a year ago, three airplanes caught fire right at their tie downs. Man, it was big. The whole sky turned red."

Trent looked at Ben.

"I thought you said the fires were caused by the sun? How could the sky turn red?"

"Well, you know, it smoldered for awhile."

"Then all three of them broke out in fire at the same time?"

The conversation was interrupted with the arrival of dinner and drinks. When everyone got their plates in front of them, the waitress returned to the dining room.

"You know," said Trent, "it's always been a custom in my family to pray before dinner. Would you guy's mind if I ask a blessing for our food?"

Before anyone could respond, Trent began to pray.

"*Oh Lord, thank you for your abundant blessings, and this food you've provided for us. I pray you will bless our time together, and enlighten us through conversation. Amen.*"

Trent could feel their eyes staring at him, and the conversation temporarily ended. But, he wanted to hear more.

"So, Ben, how did you acquire this wonderful inn? Can you earn that much money as a contract pilot?"

"You know, Trent, I think you've been playing with me. I think you know everything about me and you're beginning to piss me off."

"I don't know what you're talking about, Ben. I just got here this morning, slept all afternoon, came down for dinner and you called me over to your table."

"Look, I'll put it to you straight. I run the show here. All flying jobs around here go through me."

"Well, thanks for your services Ben, but I think I'll pass."

"You can't get fire insurance here. No one will sell it to you."

Trent was livid, but stayed cool.

"Listen, Ben. If my plane gets damaged or destroyed by any means, I'll just buy another one. If it looks like someone intentionally did this, I will reward anyone for information that'll bring the bastard to justice."

Immediately Ben got up to his feet and walked out of the cocktail lounge, followed by Bob and Rick. After Trent finished his meal, the waitress brought him the dinner check.

"I thought this was on the house?"

"Really? Ben didn't say anything to me about it."

"Well, then put it on my room tab."

The waitress took the check and left. In a few minutes she again returned.

"Honey, you don't have a room here anymore."

Beginning

It was seven o'clock when Trent opened his eyes. He was scrunched in the back seat of the Chevy which was in the parking lot in back of Scotty's office. He ached all over because of the contortions, and was badly bitten-up by the notorious Alaskan mosquitoes. He was careful to keep the doors and windows closed, but they were in the car anyway and followed the trail of carbon dioxide from his breathing.

When he left Ben's Sky Harbor on the night before, he stopped by the front desk to get his money back from the hotel receptionist. She was obviously embarrassed by giving Trent a room, and then to have her boss come along and evict him.

"I'm sorry…," she began to say.

Trent raised his hands and shook his head.

"No. No. It's not your fault. Ben just decided he didn't like me much," he had said, trying to soothe her feelings.

He got out of the car and saw Todd, the line-boy, was already getting planes out of the hanger for the students and their flight instructors that would soon be there.

He walked into the office, and saw Scotty pouring himself a cup of coffee.

"Hello, Scotty."

"Trent. You looked like you've slept in the backseat of a car."

"I did. Can I use your restroom?"

"Of course you can. What happened? Was the hotel filled?"

"I didn't try downtown. I went over to Ben's."

Trent paused a moment as he relived his experience.

"Ya know, it was like he expected me. He was just sitting in the bar, waiting for me. I remember hearing him say under his breath, 'There he is now,' to his friends when I walked into the cocktail lounge. The next thing I know he's trying to sell me some fire insurance."

Scotty listened and smiled wryly.

"Were there two guys with him?"

"Yeah. Bob and Rick."

"What we've got here is the good old fashioned shake down," said Scotty. "He calls it a union, or co-op or whatever. Anyway, no one can contract themselves out on a flying job. They all go through Ben. He takes the gravy ones for himself, and then lets the other pilots have the rest for a twenty percent fee."

"Oh, that's his game, eh? Then, when someone doesn't comply, he burns their plane."

"Exactly."

"Nice guy. How long's he been in town?"

"About ten years."

"How long has he owned the inn?"

"About three years."

"How did that happen?"

It was Scotty's turn to pause and remember past events.

"Well, I really don't know how he pulled it off, but there was a young couple that owned it before Ben. It was left to them about five years ago by the wife's parents. The kids ran it for a couple of years, and then they were both killed in a car accident. There was an estate sale and Ben got there first with the down payment."

"So, he doesn't own it outright?"

"No. But, if it becomes a burden to him, I don't think he'd hesitate to burn it down."

"Scotty, I'd like to talk to your line-boy, Todd. Would you mind if I had few words with him, privately?"

"Use my inner office. I'll get him for you."

After freshening up in the restroom, Trent sat down at Scotty's desk and in a moment Todd came in.

"You wanted to see me, Mr. Owen?"

Trent looked the young man in the eye.

"How much does Ben Barret pay you to spy for him?"

Todd's face suddenly flushed.

"I don't spy for him, Mr. Owen. I just pass on news."

"Call me Trent. I'm not angry with you, Todd. I'm just trying to figure out how things run around here. What did you tell him about me?"

"Well, I overheard you tell Scotty that you were moving here and would be working as a bush pilot."

"How much did he pay you?"

"A couple of bucks. I didn't think I was doing anything wrong."

"What did he say after you told him about me?"

"He wants me to watch you and to tell him everything you do."

"Do you mean like contracting flights?"

"Yeah, and how much people pay you."

Trent thought for a minute, and then patted the youth on the back.

"Todd, I'll make a better deal for you. I'll pay you five dollars every time you tell Ben what I want. Now you'll be making seven dollars each time you report."

Todd's eyes grew big.

"Is that legal?"

"Sure. What's the matter?"

"I donno. It just seems like there's something wrong with doing something like that."

"How about what you were doing for Ben? Do you really think that was okay?"

"Well…"

"Look, all we're doing here is leveling the playing field," said Trent. "Is there anything wrong with that?"

Todd began to buy into Trent's plan.

"Sure, I'll do it Mr…ah, Trent."

"Good. Now, don't tell anyone, even your friends about this. Okay?"

"Okay."

When they left the office, Trent saw Scotty on the phone.

"Hang on a minute," said Scotty to the caller.

"Trent, you want to fly a couple of people out to a village this afternoon?"

"Sure."

"It's a four hundred mile flight. Do you want to give them a "ballpark" on the cost?"

"Tell them I'll do it for any price they want."

Rod and Jenny

"Hello, are you our pilot?" said a voice behind Trent, as he was leaning into the cabin of his plane, collecting charts and straightening seatbelts. Turning around he was greeted by a tall, smiling man in his thirties.

"I guess so," responded Trent, returning the smile.

"I'm Rod Ames."

"I'm pleased to meet you, Rod. I'm Trent Owen." he said as they shook hands.

"Are you alone? I thought there were two passengers."

"Jenny is still shopping. She should be here soon. Scotty told me we're your first fares."

"You're not nervous, are you?"

"No, but we've got a lot of mountains here in Alaska."

Trent smiled at Rod's uneasiness.

"Don't worry. I've done tons of mountain flying. I lived in Seattle."

"We're from Seattle, too."

"What are you doing in some remote village up here?"

"Shishmar."

"What?"

"The name of the village is Shishmar. We're missionaries there."

"Really?"

"We come into the big cities every so often and do some shopping. In fact, here comes Jenny now."

A gray, battered Ford pick-up truck came out on to the flight line and stopped next to the plane, and a pert, dark haired, young woman got out of the passenger side.

"Is this our plane? Is this our pilot?" she asked Rod.

Before he could answer, she said, "C'mon, let's get this crate loaded."

"Now, just a minute. Don't you call my plane a crate," said Trent in mock anger, but still with a little edge.

"Jenny, this is Trent Owen. He's our pilot."

"Pleased to meet cha," said Jenny with a spirited grin.

"Pleased to meet you too, I think," said Trent as they shook hands.

"So how much are you charging to fly us back?"

"How much do you usually pay?"

"Well, we try to find someone between here and Shishmar. They're cheaper."

"I don't doubt that."

"We couldn't find anyone today, so I guess we're stuck with you."

Trent didn't know what to think of Jenny. While she was haggling over the fare, Rod and the young pick-up driver started loading their purchases into the baggage compartment, behind the rear seat. Trent watched them and could see they had done this before.

"So, Jenny, help me out here. How much did you pay the last time you flew from here?"

Jenny bit her lip in thought.

"It was over three hundred. We really can't afford that much."

"Well, let's see," said Trent. "It's four hundred miles, so it would take about three hours. The engine burns ten gallons per hour…hmmm. Then there's the flight back, and with the cost of gas, hmmm. And then there's oil, wear and tear on the plane, and then my fees…hmmm. Okay, I'll do it for a hundred dollars.

A glum faced Jenny, who was afraid the cost would be beyond their means, was shocked.

"What? A hundred dollars? Are you serious?"

Trent grinned at her.

"You caught me in a good mood. Excuse me. I want to talk to the line-boy."

Trent then walked up to Todd who was on a stepladder refueling a plane.

"Hi, Todd."

"Hi, Trent," the young man replied with a smile.

Trent looked around carefully, and palmed the five dollar bill he had in his pocket.

"I'm taking these people to a village, and I'm doing it for just costs. You filled my gas tanks, right?"

"Ah, yeah. I filled them last night, remember?"

"Yes, I know," said Trent, as he discretely stuffed the bill into Todd's shoe, as he stood on a ladder rung. "But, if Ben should be watching us right now, and he probably is, you can honestly tell him I asked if you serviced my plane. Then you can tell him you learned how much I was charging my fares."

His suspicions were correct. Standing on the deck of his apartment at the inn, about a third of a mile away, Ben was watching the conversation with a pair of binoculars.

Trent returned to his plane just as the pick-up truck was leaving.

"Okay you guys, climb in. I'll file a flight plan when we get into the air."

"Can I sit up front?" asked Jenny.

"Okay by me."

After everyone was settled and had their seat belts on, Trent started the engine and taxied to the end of the runway. He checked out the engine, lined up on the centerline and took off with a roar.

As they were climbing to altitude, Jenny turned in her seat and looked at Trent.

"You've got 'Anne' painted on the side of your engine. Is she your girlfriend?"

Rage

Todd watched Trent's Cessna 185 take off and turn to the northwest. He looked at his watch and noted it was 11:15 AM. He was caught up with his work, so it was a good time to break for lunch. Retrieving the five dollar bill Trent stuffed in his shoe, he decided to walk over to Ben's Sky Harbor.

After arriving, he took a seat next to a window, and placed his order for a bacon burger with cheese, fries and a strawberry shake. While waiting for his order, he heard someone come up behind him.

"Hi, Todd," said a familiar voice.

Todd turned around to see Ben Barret.

"Oh hi, Mr. Barret."

"Mind if I sit down?"

"No. Please sit down,"

"I see you're having lunch with us today," said Ben, as he slid into the booth.

"My mom forgot to make my lunch, so I'm buying today."

"Well, don't use up your college education."

"I don't think one lunch will cause that to happen," said Todd with a grin.

"I see that new guy, what's his name…?"

"Trent Owen."

"Yeah, that's it. Trent Owen. You must know him pretty good."

Todd's order arrived, interrupting the conversation.

"Well, he's buying tie-down space from my boss, Scotty, and I refueled his plane."

Ben was contemplative for a moment, and then queried Todd more.

"Where did he go today?"

"He's taking some missionaries to some Indian village," said Todd as he waded into his burger.

"Any idea what he's charging?"

"I heard he's doing it for costs."

"What? Did he tell you that?"

Todd was suddenly aware that Ben Barret was angry. He remembered Trent telling him to be careful and not to let anyone know of their alliance.

"Uh, I heard Trent talking to the missionaries, and he said he would make the flight for costs only."

Ben flew into a rage.

"That bastard! That son-of-a-bitch!" he roared.

He leaped to his feet and stomped out of the dining room. Other diners, including Todd were startled by the outburst.

Ben went directly to his office, picked up the phone and dialed a number.

"Anchorage Flight Control Center," answered a voice.

"This is Ben Barret."

"Hi, Mr. Barret. Would you like to file a flight plan?"

"No. But, we just had a plane depart Merrill Field. Could you tell me his destination?"

"What time did he leave Merrill?"

"About an hour ago. In a Cessna 185."

"That would be Trent Owen. He's on a flight to the village of Shishmar."

"Where's that?"

"It's on the coast about 400 miles northwest of Anchorage."

"Thanks."

Ben hung up and then quickly called another number.

"Hello?"

"Bob? It's Ben."

"Hi, Ben."

"I need you and your Cessna 210."

"You got me a fare?"

"Yeah. Me. Hustle over here. I'll meet you at your plane."

Ben hung up the phone and went to the gun case on the office wall. After opening the lock, he selected a Winchester .308 rifle and took it with him out the door.

Flight to Shishmar

While climbing out from Merrill Field, Trent keyed his microphone.

"Anchorage Flight Control Center, this is Cessna 2446 Juliet, I'd like to open a flight plan from Merrill Field to the village of Shishmar."

"Roger, Juliet. How many people?"

"I have three souls onboard. Estimate three hours enroute and I have fuel for five hours."

"Roger, Juliet. Have a nice day."

Jenny wasn't going to let an interruption get in the way of her quest.

"Who's Anne? Why's her name painted on the engine cowl?"

Trent almost felt trod upon by this innocent young woman's curiosity.

"She was my wife."

"Was?"

"She's dead. I accidentally killed her with this plane."

"Oh, I'm sorry. Please forgive me for being so stupid."

Jenny put her hands to her face and began to cry.

"I thought I was going to hear a happy story. I should learn to mind my business."

Trent felt her honest despair.

"It's okay, Jenny. I'm getting over it."

She took a handkerchief out of her pocket, wiped her eyes and blew her nose then silently watched the puffy clouds go by her window. Then she turned to Trent.

"What happened?"

Trent looked at her again.

"Jenny, I'll tell you the whole story someday."

Rod couldn't hear their conversation from the backseat because of the engine noise, but knowing his wife, he was afraid she was pestering Trent with her active mind.

"Jenny, just watch the scenery. It's beautiful," he called out to her.

The weather was perfect. They'd been in the air over two and a half hours, above a mountainous wilderness that stretched in all directions.

Boy, I'd hate to lose an engine about now, thought Trent.

There were inherent dangers of flying over this kind of terrain. It would take a miracle to find you if you went down. There were many Alaskan fliers that simply vanished.

"Do you have any children?" asked Jenny.

Trent had been lost in thought.

"What?"

"I said, do you have any children?"

"Yes, I have a son and a daughter."

"Is someone taking care of them while you're here?"

Trent turned and looked at Jenny. Here was a beautiful young woman who had dedicated her life for others. She was worried that Trent may have abandoned his children by trying to run away from pain. He loved her for her honest concern.

"They're both in college."

Trent turned back again, to face the instruments.

"Oh," she replied.

"How long have you and Rod been in this village?" asked Trent.

"One year."

"What exactly do you do?"

"Rod is working on a program to help the people deal with alcohol. You know, that's a big problem with Indians."

"So I've heard."

"They think it might be a genetic problem, but no one knows for sure."

"Are these Indians the same as Eskimos?"

"They are really Inuits, but in some areas they are called Eskimos. They all came across the land bridge from Siberia."

"What do you do, Jenny?"

"I try to be a friend to the women. They're left alone a lot and need companionship. So I organize get-togethers at the village meeting hall. We have games for the kids and Bible readings. Then on Sundays, we hold church services and Rod preaches the sermons."

"I see the coast, we must be there," said Trent.

"Yes. The village is right below us."

It was located next to the protected waters of a small bay that opened onto the Bering Straits. Trent looked around for a place to land.

"Where is the airstrip?"

Rod leaned forward pointing to the east of the village.

"There's a short strip there, but since the permafrost is melting, it's just a muddy mess."

"I see there's a dock on the bay. I'll make a water landing and tie up there."

"Whoa," said Jenny. "I thought this was a land airplane. I mean we took off from an airport."

Trent grinned at her.

"This plane is an amphibian. It can land on water or land."

He made a low pass over the water to look for rocks and partially sunken logs. Seeing none, he landed on the water and taxied up to the dock.

The people from the village came down to the water. Jenny stepped up on to the dock and was immediately overwhelmed by both the adults and the children. Trent and Rod pulled everything out of the baggage compartment and handed it to the men who had come to help. Soon everything was out of the plane.

"Do you need some gas to get back to Anchorage, Trent?" asked Rod.

"Yeah, I could use about fifteen gallons."

Rod spoke to someone on the dock and they brought three five gallon jerry cans of fuel. Someone else came up with a funnel. Trent stood on the dock railing and with a little help, refueled the right wing tank. After securing the cap, he jumped down from the railing and said his good-by. Both Rod and Jenny hugged him as well as some of the villagers. He climbed down onto the left pontoon, untied the tether, and opened the cabin door.

"Wait!" Rod suddenly called out. "I forgot to pay you."

"Forget it," he called back with a grin. "The fifteen gallons of gas is payment enough for me."

Then he climbed into the cabin and shut the door. With a small push on the wing by Rod, the plane drifted away from the dock. Trent started the engine and made his take-off run toward the open sea.

Canyon

"He must be around here somewhere," said Ben as he swiveled his head back and forth to look out of the windshield and side window.

Just then, the radio crackled.

"Anchorage Center, this is Cessna 2446 Juliet."

"Go ahead, Juliet," answered Anchorage.

"I'm 270 miles from Anchorage inbound on the 310 radial."

"Roger. We'll expect another position report from you in one hour."

Ben couldn't believe his luck. Trent just announced his location.

"I see him!" shouted Bob.

"He's about two thousand feet below us."

"Let me have the controls."

Bob looked nervously at Ben.

"What are ya gonna do, shoot him?"

"We gotta do something, Bob, or he'll put us outta business."

Ben put his plane into a dive to build up airspeed. He was closing in from Trent's eleven o'clock position at over 200 miles an hour. Trent didn't even see them coming as they flashed over his windshield within a whisker of hitting it. Instinctively, Trent jinked his plane to the right to avoid a collision.

Ben climbed above Trent, and laughed.

"Look at 'im. He's looking all over trying to figure out what happened."

"Jeez, Ben. Ya scared the hell outta me. What are ya trying to do?"

He ignored the question.

"Here, Bob, you take the controls a minute."

Ben reached for his rifle lying on the backseat. He cranked a live round into the chamber and unlatched his door. He held it open against the slipstream with his knee enough to poke out his rifle barrel. They were over the top and behind Trent's plane.

"Bob, pick up some speed and get a little ahead of him so I can take a shot."

"No. I'm not gonna let you do that."

"You do as I say, or I'll use this bullet on you!"

As they slid forward, they could see Trent spotted them, but too late to realized he was about to be shot at.

Bang.

Trent was at point blank range and the bullet penetrated the left wing fuel tank. A spume of gasoline began to come out of the hole.

As he again made a sharp turn to the right, he picked up his microphone.

"Cessna 46 Juliet to Center."

"Go ahead, Juliet."

"I'm being attacked by another plane!"

"What? What kind of plane?"

"It's a Cessna 210."

"What's he doing?"

"He gave me a really close buzz job, and I think he's shooting at me."

"Any ID?"

"Negative. He's too fast for me to get his numbers."

"What's your location now?"

"I'm a few miles to the southeast of my last position report. I'm descending closer to the terrain. Maybe that'll help."

"He's probably listening to us," said the controller.

"You bet we are!" roared Ben. "Let me have the controls again. I'm gonna follow him down."

Ben stayed close behind Trent, who was diving for the safety of hills, ridges or anything he could put between him and his attacker.

"I think he'll be outta fuel before he can make it back to Anchorage, but just to be sure, I'm gonna try to clip his tail feathers."

Trent descended into a large canyon that meandered through snow capped peaks. Ben and Bob, in the Cessna 210, were directly behind him and gaining. Ben was trying to get close enough to tick the rudder of the Cessna 185, to throw it out of control.

Trent flew down the center of the canyon and watched its stone walls become higher and closer together. After making one more turn, he suddenly saw the blind end. Directly in front of him was a sloping wall of stone, mostly covered by a white pristine glacier with deep blue crevasses.

Acting instantly, Trent pulled back sharply on the controls. The plane almost stood on its tail. He could feel it shake as the wing stalled out. He saw the Cessna 210 go beneath him as he pushed hard on the left rudder pedal causing his plane to roll on to its back. Now inverted and keeping the control wheel pulled back into his stomach, the plane fell into the bottom half of a loop, or "Split-S", and he was able to bring it back to level flight only two hundred feet above the canyon floor and in the opposite direction.

Ben was close behind the Cessna 185, when it suddenly went vertical. Taken completely by surprise he shot past him.

Looking back, his last words were, "What the hell's he doing?"

It was Bob's cry that caused him to look forward again. Just in time to see the windshield fill with white and blue.

The Cessna 210 hit the glacier at an angle and then slid on the ice uphill to a waiting crevasse. The burning wreckage fell hundreds of feet into the chasm.

Inquiry

After returning to Merrill Field, Trent landed and taxied up to the gas pit where a small crowd was waiting for him. He was still shaken by the ordeal, and slowly opened the cabin door and stepped out onto the left pontoon.

"Trent, what the hell happened?" shouted out Scotty.

A State Police car rolled up and a tall trooper got out. Even Todd, the line-boy was there as well as several of the local pilots, including Rick Manus.

The trooper took things in hand.

"I want all you people who have no business here to clear out!"

They all backed away. Some left the area, while others watched from a distance.

"Scotty, can we use your office?" asked the trooper. "I need to take a statement."

"Sure. Of course."

They walked into the office and sat down at a table. Scotty brought in the coffee pot and some mugs.

"Scotty, I want you to join us too. You're here all of the time. Maybe you could help shed some light on this."

"Okay."

The trooper had a clipboard with a yellow tablet, which he laid on the table in front of him. Trent was seated directly across the table and Scotty sat at the end.

"Mr. Owen, I'm Sergeant Mike Ashcroft of the State Police, and I'd like you to tell me what happened."

The sergeant poised over the pad with a pen.

Trent was still shaking and tried to collect his wits.

"How do you know my name?"

"The Flight Control Center gave us your name and said you had been attacked by another plane."

"Uh, well, everything happened so fast."

"What happened?"

"I was flying on a course to Anchorage. I was about an hour out from an Indian village on the coast."

"Yes." Said the sergeant, as he wrote on his pad. "Go on."

"Well, suddenly something flew at me a little left from head on."

"Did you see what it was?"

"No. At first I thought it was an eagle. I instinctively turned the plane to the right and got off my course. I was about to turn back to the left and then I saw another plane directly above me."

The sergeant was writing furiously to keep up with the story.

"Did you see what kind of plane it was?" asked the trooper.

"Yes. It was a red and white Cessna 210."

"You're sure about that?"

"Yes. And then I saw the barrel of a rifle sticking out from the door, and I saw it fire."

"Then what happened?"

"I tried to get away by diving into a canyon."

"And he followed you?"

"I think so. The next thing I knew, I was in a blind canyon with a glacier dead ahead."

"And then?"

"I did a Split-S maneuver to take me out of there. Then I got back on a heading to Anchorage."

"Did you see the other Cessna again?"

"Just briefly as he passed beneath me."

"When he fired at you, do you think he hit your plane?"

"He hit my left fuel tank. I began losing gas fast enough I could see the needle go down. Luckily, I topped off the right tank in the Indian village, so I had enough to get me back."

"So that's the whole story?"

"I think so."

"Scotty, do you have any comments?"

"Yeah. Plenty. Bob Cannon has a red and white Cessna 210, and he's a pal of Ben Barret."

"Is his plane on the field?"

"Not now it ain't. Todd saw them take off a few hours ago with Ben, and he was carrying a rifle."

"That's not unusual, is it Scotty? I mean, a lot of bush pilots carry a rifle in their planes," commented the trooper.

"Maybe so, but not Ben. He doesn't even fly much anymore since he's been running his inn and his extortion racket."

"Hold on Scotty, no one's ever proved he was behind those airplane fires," said the sergeant hotly.

"That's because no one would ever stand up to him. They're all scared. Besides he's got some politicians in his pocket."

The trooper shrugged and shook his head.

"C'mon Scotty. How would he ever find Trent out there? Why would he do something like this?"

"Cause I wouldn't play ball with him," said Trent.

"You mean he threatened you?"

"Sort of. He wanted me to join his club, where he gets twenty percent of my fares, or something would happen to my plane. I told him to go to hell."

"That doesn't prove anything."

"But, he did know that Trent flew to Shishmar," said Scotty.

"How?" asked the trooper.

"Because Todd, my line-boy, told him."

"What?"

"I paid Todd five bucks to tell him," added Trent.

"You mean you tried to set him up to do this?"

"I had no idea he'd do something like this. I was trying to get his goat by telling him I was flying my own fares, and at my price. In this case it was only for costs."

The trooper sat quietly thinking for a moment.

"Still, how could he find you?" he asked.

"I gave a position report every hour. I'd say it would be easy."

"Man, this guy is a pillar of the community," said the Trooper. "He hobnobs with everyone important. I mean this is a big deal. I guess I'll have to hang around until he gets back and talk to him."

"If he followed me into that canyon, he's not coming back."

Winter

"Man. It's cold," said Trent, as he stomped the snow from his boots and entered Scotty's pilot's lounge.

"Aw, yer just a big sissy," teased Scotty. "It's only twenty below. Wait 'til it really gets cold. What are ya doing out here on a day like this, anyway? You ain't gonna fly are ya?"

"My church gotta message from a village about 250 miles northeast of here. One of their kids is sick. I'm taking Doc Watson with me."

After losing Ann, he wanted to live a life of service, dedicated to the memory of his wife. He joined a Presbyterian Church and became active as a deacon and an elder.

"Yer crazy. You'll end up like Ben."

They never did find Ben, or Bob who disappeared in the Alaskan wilderness. No one knew they ended up inside a deep crevasse on a nameless glacier at the end of a nameless canyon.

"No, I won't. Look here," said Trent as he unfolded a sectional chart of the area.

"If I fly outbound on the 30 degree radial, I'll pass right over the village."

As he spoke he traced the route with his finger.

"And right there," he poked the map with his finger, "is the landing strip."

"So, how are ya gonna land while it's snowing and ya can't see anything?"

"I called up the flight center and they said the weather was clear at the village."

Just then, Doc burst through the door.

"Man, its cold out there."

"Aw, ya big sissy," said Trent.

"How will you see where you're going?"

"I'll dodge the flakes."

Doc looked dubiously at him.

"Okay, then," said Trent, "I'll use the instruments."

"How about when we get there? How will you find the airport?"

"The weathers good there. You don't want to wait 'til tomorrow, do you?" asked Trent.

"No. The kid's pretty sick. She might not last 'til then."

Trent picked up his plane's battery from a back room where it was stored to keep from freezing and carried it out to the plane. He had the floats removed and replaced with skis at the first sign of snow. They were a type that allowed the landing gear wheel to extend through them so he could also use concrete runways.

They climbed into the plane, started the engine, and began taxiing to the end of the runway.

"Anchorage Flight Center, this is Cessna 2446 Juliet," Trent announced into his microphone.

"Go ahead, Juliet."

"I want to open a flight plan to the village of Umvic; that's 250 miles out bound from Merrill Field on the 30 degree radial."

"46 Juliet, we show Merrill as below minimums for take-off."

"I know, but there's a kid that might die if we wait for the weather to clear."

There was a few seconds pause while the flight controllers had a conference.

"46 Juliet, I can't give you permission to take off. It's against the regs."

"I'm not asking for permission. I'm telling you what I'm going to do."

"What if you take-off and hit some other plane trying to land?"

"Do you think there's anyone stupid enough to be out in weather like this?"

"No."

"Okay then. There are two of us on board and I'm climbing to 10,000 feet to assure terrain clearance."

"The wind is from the north at twenty. Contact us when you break out, or if you break out."

"46 Juliet is standing by on this frequency."

Trent looked at Doc with a grin.

"They're not too happy, are they?"

Doc was scared to death, but he trusted Trent.

After checking out the engine instruments, controls and setting the altimeter, Trent moved to the approximate middle of the runway. By watching his gyro-compass, he turned the plane onto the centerline heading which was about northwest.

"I can't see a thing out there," said Doc.

"Here we go!"

The engine roar was deafening. There was no sensation of speed except for the slight "G" force against the seat backs. Trent was glued to the gyros and then felt the plane break free from the ground

As they climbed, he made a shallow turn to the right until he saw the Omni needle began to move. Gradually, he adjusted his heading until he was on course.

"How high are we?" asked Doc.

"Were at three thousand and still climbing. We're on our way to ten thousand."

The plane began to buck.

"What's that?" cried Doc.

"Just some turbulence. They're updrafts caused by the wind rolling over mountain ridges and peaks."

"You sure were not going to hit one?"

"Yep."

They continued on there course for another twenty minutes when they suddenly broke out into the clear. The mountains laden with fresh snow gleamed in the sunlight. The sky was a dark blue that contrasted with the white peaks.

"Hey, Trent, some of the mountain tops are higher than we are."

"Yeah, but we didn't hit them, did we?"

"I want to know why?"

"Because they are not on our path. If we'd strayed we'd be dead. Which reminds me, I forgot to call Center."

"Anchorage Flight Center, this is 46 Juliet. We're out of the clouds and about an hour from our destination."

"Whew. We were getting worried," replied the controller.

"We've got it made now. 46 Juliet, out."

Trent began a shallow descent, and later they spotted the village that was located on a tributary of the Tanana River. The airstrip was outlined by cut bushes, sleds, blankets and anything else that would show up on the snow. They even had made an arrow showing the direction they should land.

He made a pass and everyone came running. He circled around, lined-up with the marked strip and landed. As he taxied toward the small crowd, he could see the expectant look on their faces. He shut down the engine and they opened their doors to a cold blast of air.

Fever

Doc got his kit out of the backseat of the plane, and together with Trent, faced the welcoming committee. No one said a word.
"Do you speak English?" asked Trent.
"Of course we speak English," said one of the men.
"You need a doctor?"
"Yes. My daughter is very sick."
Now the speaker came forward.
"My name is Trent, and this is Doc Watson."
"My name is Jacob," said the man as he came up to them.
"What's wrong with your daughter?" asked Doc.
"She's sick."
"Can I see her?"
"Yes. Follow me."
The crowd moved to allow a pathway. Jacob looked to be about thirty-five, dark, with black hair. He was robust and probably a good hunter and provider.
He led them to a small shack that could hardly keep the wind out, let alone the cold. Inside was a cot covered with a bearskin. A small oil burning lamp was the only source of light when the door was closed. A woman, probably the mother, sat next to the cot.
Doc pulled back the bearskin and saw two black shiny button eyes staring up at him, wide with fright.
"Hi there. What's your name?"
"Her name is, Kirima," said Jacob.

"How old are you, Kirima?"
"She's six."
Doc looked at Jacob.
"Can she talk?"
"Not now." A tear trickle down the crease between his nose and cheek.
"Do you mean she won't talk?"
"Yes."
Doc looked at Trent.
"She's got a hell of a fever. I don't need to take her temperature." He pulled a small flashlight out of his kit.
"Kirima, can you open your mouth for me?"
She slowly shook her head.
"I just want to see your throat. That's all."
"Jacob, ask her to open her mouth."
"Kirima, open your mouth."
She shook her head.
Doc was stymied. He decided to try the angry approach.
"Kirima! Open your mouth!" he shouted.
No way would she do it.
"Doc, we gotta get out of here. There's not much daylight left," said Trent.
"One more try."
He reached into his kit and pulled out a large hypodermic needle.
"You see this?" he said as he held it in front of her face.
Her eyes were really big now.
"Look how long it is, and how sharp. Now, I'm going to stick your arm, and the needle's so long it'll go all of the way through."
"No, Doc! No!" cried Jacob.
"Keep him away, Trent."
Trent took Jacob's arm
"Here it comes!" shouted Doc as he scratched her arm.
"Yiiiiiiiiiiiiii!" screamed the girl.
He was quick and grabbed her open jaw, and with his light was able to look into her mouth and throat.

"Oh, my God!"

"What is it, Doc!" cried Trent.

He took Trent aside.

"It's typhoid. Typhoid fever."

"What should we do?" asked Trent, now seeing the alarmed expression on Doc's face.

"Can you call out on your radio?"

"I don't know. I might reach Anchorage Center."

"Tell them to contact the State Department of Health, and that we've got a typhoid case here. They'll know what to do."

"Can't we just fly her out of here to a hospital?"

"Were not going anywhere. We're stuck here until this thing is over."

"What about the girl?"

"She won't make it through the night."

"Poor Jacob."

"You get on the radio. I'll break the news to Jacob."

Trent managed to reach Anchorage Flight Control Center and relay Doc's orders in time before the battery failed from the cold. As he walked back toward the shack, he could hear Kirima's parents mournful cries as they mingled with the moaning wind.

Cold

"I got a message through before the battery went dead," said Trent to Doc, who was talking with one of the men.

"Good. Someone should be here tomorrow with vaccine. They'll probably bring in a Snowcat."

Doc then introduced Trent to the pastor of the Russian Orthodox Church.

"This is Father Joseph. He's gonna show us where we'll spend the night."

"Hello, Father."

Father Joseph was an Inuit. He was in his thirties and had a pleasant expression. Most of the native people looked serious or sad.

"Hello, Trent. Thank you for coming. I'll show you where you'll stay."

They followed the Father to a small church building. On entering, they went into a single room with two army cots and two oil lamps, already burning.

"I'll bring in some of our dogs. They'll curl up with you and keep you warm."

"They don't have fleas, do they?" asked Trent.

Father Joseph grinned at him and shook his head.

"Fleas? Here? No, no."

Trent wondered if he'd asked the wrong question.

"My family and I live next door. We would be pleased to have you join us for supper."

"That's very nice of you to invite us, Father," said Doc. "We'd be delighted."

"Good. Come over around six o'clock," said Father Joseph and then he left them.

"We don't have to eat with them. I've got provisions in the plane."

Doc smiled and put his hand on Trent's shoulder.

"I know you do, but it would be terribly rude to refuse him. Put yourself in his shoes. He doesn't get many chances to be a host to someone outside the village. These people are proud and they want to do something to make us feel welcomed. They're not gonna pay us."

"I see your point, Doc. I just hope grilled dog isn't on the menu."

"Nah. They wouldn't do that."

"I've got to go back to the plane and bring in the battery. Why don't you go with me, Doc? You can bring in a couple of sleeping bags."

The plane was resting about a hundred yards from the village, and even though it was only five o'clock in the afternoon, there wasn't a ray of sun left to be seen. They had their parka hoods up over their heads with its soft fur pulled tightly around their faces.

"Man is it cold!" cried Trent.

"It's at least minus thirty," said Doc. "We've got a pretty strong wind too. Aren't you worried the wind might blow the plane away?"

"It's not going anywhere. The skis are frozen to the ground. I'm gonna tie down the tail though. A strong gust might flip it over."

"Look at the stars."

"Yeah. They seem to come all the way down to the ground."

After stepping away from the buildings, they could see the northern lights ruling the sky.

"I've never seen them like this. Look how bright they are. And, all of the colors."

"You know," said Doc, "some people claim they can actually hear them."

"Really?"

"Yeah. Trappers who are alone and miles from any civilization have said they can."

"What do they sound like?"

"They say they sound like chimes."

"Maybe they hear voices too," joked Trent. "C'mon. It's too cold to stand here and talk."

When they got to the plane, Trent opened the aft baggage compartment, and pulled out a small maul and a steel stake. He hammered the stake into the permafrost just behind the tail-wheel, and secured it with a short length of cable. Doc gathered up two compacted, down sleeping bags. Trent put away the maul, and removed the plane's storage battery. After closing up the doors, they trekked back to the church.

"These oil lamps give off a little heat," said Trent. "Maybe there's enough warmth in here to revive the battery."

"Well, let's hope so," remarked Doc. "It's a quarter of six, why don't we go on over to Father Joseph's house."

Father Joseph's home, like the others in the villages, were made of rough hewn cedar. Through the window, they could see the soft glow of oil lamps. Doc rapped softly.

"Come in, come in." said Father Joseph on opening the door.

In the dim light, they could see the outline of his wife and three curious kids, two girls and a boy.

"Helen, this is Trent and Doc."

"Hello," said Helen, who approached with a smile. She was an attractive Inuit, and like Father Joseph, obviously educated.

"We are so pleased to have you stay with us," she said.

"We are happy to be included in your family," responded Doc.

"Supper will be ready soon," she said returning to preparing the meal. "Father Joseph, pour them a glass of sherry to warm them up."

He produce a bottle of Harvey's Bristol Crème Sherry and announced, "This occasion calls for the good stuff.

Looking around through the lamp smoke, Trent could see it was a large room with one large bed, probably for the children. There were two other adjoining rooms. One, with a door, was probably the toilet, and the other was the master bedroom.

The men sat down at a table, the children were on the floor playing with toys, and using crayons in a coloring book. This was only the second time Trent visited an Alaskan native village. The first was when he flew the missionaries, Rod and Jenny, to Shishmar last summer.

"Where did you go to school, Father Joseph?" asked Trent

"I studied sociology at the University of Washington, and then went to seminary."

"Really? Why do you have a Russian church here?"

Father Joseph thought before answering.

"Remember, Alaska was originally owned by the Russians. Many churches were founded by Russian missionaries, and they're operating today."

"Time to eat," said Helen as she brought a platter of smoked salmon to the table.

They spent the evening learning about each other and their life styles.

"That was a wonderful supper," said Doc. Then turning to Father Joseph, "We'll need your help tomorrow. A team of medical workers will come in and will want to inoculate every one. I know some of the people will be resistant, but if they don't take the shot, they could become carriers.

Father Joseph looked at his own children, who were now lying on top of their bed. Then he looked at Doc with a serious expression.

"I'll do what I can."

"Good. I'm counting on you to convince the others to comply. Or, we'll be back again, and it might not be for just one little girl."

They said goodnight to Helen, and then walked with Father Joseph back to the church.

"Go on in, I'll get a couple of the dogs for you."

He came in with two Siberian huskies and then returned to his home.

After crawling into their sleeping bags, the dogs obediently jumped up and lay down on top of them. The body heat they generated was almost too much.

A few hours later, Trent was awakened by Doc fussing about something.
"What's the matter, Doc?"
"You know what they feed these dogs?"
"Dog food?"
"Fish. I'd rather put up with fleas. They're gonna gas us to death."

Body Snatchers

Trent awakened and looked at the illuminated dial of his watch. Eight o'clock.

He no longer could feel the weight of the dog that kept him warm during the night. Looking through the haze of the oil lamps, he could see Doc's bed was now empty. Crawling out of his sleeping bag, he got to his feet and relieved himself in the provided receptacle. He put on his insulated boots and parka and then opened the door.

Instantly, he was met by a blast of cold air, and a sky full of stars. In the distance, he could hear voices and engine noises. Walking toward the commotion, he saw vehicle headlights on the frozen river, coming toward the village. He nearly walked into Doc who was standing on the river bank.

"Mornin', Trent."

"What's going on?"

"The Snowcats are here with the public health team."

"Why didn't you wake me?"

"We might be able to fly out of here today. I want to be sure you're good and rested before I fly with you again. You scared the hell outta me with your blind take-off from Anchorage," said Doc, half in jest.

"So what's gonna happen?"

"The teams are gonna inoculate everyone, including you and me, and they're gonna stick around for a few days to see if anyone else gets sick."

Sunrise made its appearance around ten o'clock. With help from Father Joseph, the efficient team had the people in a serpentine line that went through the village meeting center.

One of the medical team members, a young woman, walked up to Trent and Doc.

"You guys probably still have typhoid immunity, but I'd better inoculate you too, just to be on the safe side."

The two men took off their parkas, and rolled up their sleeves. It only took a few seconds.

"Did you find anyone else sick?" asked Doc, as he again donned his parka.

"No. So far, the little girl is the only one. Hard to say how she contracted it. Maybe a carrier passed through the village."

The young woman paused a minute.

"You don't have to stay here. You can go back to Anchorage."

She paused again as if she had something difficult on her mind. Then she looked at Trent.

"You're the pilot?"

"Yeah."

"We would like you to take the girls body with you."

"Whoa. Is that safe?"

"We'll put her in a sealed bag. The thing is, she can still be infectious to anyone who's not protected. So she'll have to be taken out of here."

Trent looked at Doc, who nodded in agreement.

"We've got to do this, Trent. She's gotta be cremated right away."

"A funeral home in Anchorage will be notified," said the woman. "They'll be waiting for you at the airport."

"Her parents agree to this?"

The health worker looked down, and then back at Trent.

"They won't go along with this. It's their custom to let the body freeze, and then bury it when they can dig a hole in the permafrost."

"So, how are you going to do this? How will you take that little girl's body away from her parents?"

"Get your plane all ready to go and we'll handle it." Then she walked away.

Trent was beside himself.

"Doc, I don't want any part of this."

"I know how you feel, Trent. But, it's gotta be done."

"When my wife was killed, it took me years to begin to recover. I still haven't gotten through it."

"You never will."

"And, now this. Why can't they take her back in one of the Snowcats?"

"They might not leave the village for days. That girl's body is like a time bomb waiting to go off, possibly spreading the disease to other villages by unsuspecting victims passing through here."

Trent turned and walked back to the church building. He picked up the storage battery and was about to carry it to the plane when Father Joseph entered the room.

"Trent, I want to thank you again for helping us."

He set the battery on a chair.

"We didn't do much. Just the one girl was sick, and she died before we could do anything."

"But, you did help us. You got the medical team to come out here, and now you're going to take away a source of the infection so others won't get sick."

"I feel so bad for the girl's mom and dad. What a dreadful thing to do to them."

Father Joseph was quiet for a moment.

"Trent, you're not used to death like we are."

"Not used to it?" Trent said loudly. "I killed my wife! I have to live every day with that. I can't get over it."

Father Joseph now understood why Trent was taking this so badly.

"It was an accident?"

"Yes. Of course. A terrible accident and it was my fault."

"We have accidents. We have sickness. Our people are dying all of the time. We all die. The difference is we live with death. We don't have professionals, who come in and deprive us of handling our dead, and allowing us to grieve and get over it. Your people are insulated from that, and if you can't come to terms with it, you'll never get over it."

Then he left.

Trent was numb. He sat down on the bed. He thought he was through his grief, but it all came rushing back. For ten minutes he emptied his very soul. When he was finished, he picked up the battery and took it to the plane.

He then saw Doc coming with the sleeping bags, and his medical kit. Doc put things away in the baggage compartment, while Trent secured the battery and fastened the leads. He removed the cable from the tail-wheel and tried to pull up the stake it was attached to, but permafrost won the tug-of-war.

The young woman from the medical team came up to them.

"All ready to go?"

"Just about. We'll see if there's enough juice in the battery to start the engine."

"We'll bring out the girls body after you get the engine started," she said, and then returned to the village.

Trent climbed into the pilot's seat and looked at his friend.

"Well, Doc. Here goes nothin'."

He set the mixture control to full rich, gave the engine a couple of shots of prime, and engaged the starter. The battery was weak, but the engine caught and roared to life.

Doc leaned into the cabin.

"How ya gonna get the skis unfrozen from the ground!" he shouted above the engine noise.

"Stand back and I'll show ya!"

Trent revved the engine to full power and pushed the control wheel slightly forward. The blast from the propeller hit the elevators and raised the tail up from the ground. He quickly pulled back on the controls and the tail slammed down. The skis were still frozen, and the plane didn't budge. He tried it again and this time the skis broke free, and the plane lurched forward about twenty feet.

Doc ran up to the plane and shouted, "Here they come!"

It was a pathetic sight. One of the men of the health care team came running toward the plane, with a package in his arms. He was closely followed by the dead girl's father, who caught up to him and tripped him up.

The father was screaming, "No, no you can't take her away!"

Other men, including Father Joseph, were struggling with the distraught man, trying to hold him back. Finally, the man who was tripped got up, picked up the package and this time made it to the plane. Doc took the package from him and shoved it into the back seat, and then climbed into the front.

Trent didn't bother with the usual engine and controls check. He shoved the throttle all the way forward and prayed there wasn't something under the snow that would catch a ski. The plane obediently leaped into the sky and they were on there way back to Anchorage.

The weather was clear all the way. No nasty snow and clouds to contend with, which was a relief to Doc. After landing at Merrill Field, Trent taxied to the gas pit and immediately saw a panel truck drive up.

"Are you Trent?" called out the driver.

"Yes."

"I'm supposed to pick up a package."

"It's in the backseat."

Doc got out and helped load the body into the van. He climbed in too, and then they left.

"Glad to see you again, Trent," said Todd, the line boy. When you took off yesterday morning, you went right over a line of parked planes. I don't know how you missed them."

"You wanna earn another five bucks, Todd?"

"Sure. What'd ya want me to do?"

"Don't tell anyone about it. Especially Doc."

He reached in his wallet and fished out a five, and gave it to Todd.

Then he walked up to the front of the plane and looked at the name he'd painted on the cowling, so he'd never forget.

Anne.

He put his hand on the name and caressed it.

Then he walked into Scotty's pilot lounge.

"Hi, Trent. Good to see you back."

"Scotty, I want to get a new paint job on my plane."

"Sure, I can arrange that."

"Remember the red and white paint scheme Bob Cannon hand on his Cessna 210?"

"Yeah."

"Make it like that."

"Okay. And do you want to keep the name, Anne, on the cowling?"

"No. I want it painted over."

Bank

A few days later, Trent walked in the pilot lounge door and started scuffing his boots on the floor mat.

"Guess what?" said Scotty.

"What?"

"The bank's put up Ben's Sky Harbor for sale."

"So, why don't you by it?"

"I would if I had the money. They've always had a good business," Scotty said with a little controlled excitement. "Why don't you go over to the bank and see Tom?"

"C'mon, Scotty. What would I do with a thing like that?"

"I dunno. I thought you might like to check it out?"

Trent learned somewhere back in his life not to brush off unsolicited advice.

"Okay, Scotty. I'll talk to him."

He didn't have anything special to do this day, so he drove over to the bank, which was in downtown Anchorage.

As he entered the main door, he stepped into a bank robbery.

There were two slightly built men, maybe teenagers, with ski masks, and they already had their loot in paper bags. They were heading toward the door, and in their blind rush, did not see Trent coming through the entrance. The first man ran right into him.

"Hey! What the hell's going on?" shouted Trent.

"Outta my way! Outta my way!" yelled the bandit as he tried to bring his pistol around.

Trent immediately grabbed the gun away from the robber and struck him unconscious with it. The second man ran into the first man and seeing Trent, who now had a pistol in his hand, dropped his gun and gave up.

A big commotion followed. Alarms went off, customers and bank employees jumped on the robbers, and some of them ran up to Trent and hugged him.

"Wow!" said Tom Anderson, as he rushed up excitedly, and put an arm around Trent. "You just took out two bad guys all by yourself."

Trent was still in a daze as everything happened so fast. He looked down at the young man lying on the floor in a pool of blood around his head. Someone had removed their ski masks and they could see the young men were Inuits.

"I just hope I didn't kill that kid."

"Don't worry about it. He would have killed you, if he could," said Tom.

Then the police came and closed the bank. They handcuffed the robber who gave up and took him away, but they had to call an ambulance for the other one who was still unconscious.

Both Tom and Trent were questioned by the police about what they saw and did.

"Now, when you hit the kid," asked detective Murphy, "did you try to kill him?"

"No! I dunno! Look, all I saw was a guy with a gun. I don't know how I got the gun away from him. Everything happened so fast. All I remember is I ended up holding the gun by the barrel, and the kid…I mean robber, was lying on the floor."

"We've got a little problem," said Murphy. "If you had the gun, then he's no longer a threat. It might be hard to prove you didn't use excessive force."

"Excessive force? There were two of them. They both had guns. What should I have done? Just stand there and let them kill me? If I wanted to use excessive force, I'd have used the other end of the gun."

"I know, I know. I don't have a problem with that. It's the prosecutor. He's the one who might bring charges."

"Charges? What kind of charges?"

Murphy looked down at the floor, and then directly into Trent's eyes.

"If the kid recovers, probably nothing will come of it. If he dies, you might be tried for manslaughter. Ya see, there's two kinds of law up here. One that protects the natives, and one for everyone else."

Finally, after two hours the police left, and Tom decided to close the bank for the rest of the day.

"C'mon, Trent, I'll buy you lunch."

Tom drove Trent over to the Sky Harbor Inn, and they were shown to a table at the restaurant. Trent was still upset about the warning given by the police officer.

"Can they do that, Tom? Can they really hold me responsible if that robber dies?"

Tom shrugged his shoulders. "I dunno, Trent. But, because you stopped the holdup, we'll back you with our whole legal staff."

They ordered sandwiches and beer, then Trent remembered the reason he went to see Tom at the bank in the first place.

"Have you had any nibbles on selling the inn?"

"As a matter of fact, I have," said Tom, as he leaned back in his chair. "But, I don't think she's gonna qualify."

"She?" asked Trent with raised eyebrows.

"Yeah. A young couple had the place before Ben, and they were killed in a car accident."

"I heard about that. What happened?"

"They went off the road and down a steep embankment."

"Anyone see it happen?"

"No one will say they had."

"How did Ben end up with the inn?"

Tom paused a moment to remember.

"Well, it should have gone to the closest living relative, but somehow that was waived and we, the bank, put it up for sale. Ben got it for just making the payments."

They stopped talking when the waitress brought their lunch.

"Will that be all?" she asked.

"Bring us a couple more beers," said Tom.

When she was out of earshot, their conversation continued.

"So lemme see if I've got this," said Trent looking at Tom. "The owners were killed, and the hotel and restaurant were bought by Ben for resuming payments on the original loan."

"That's it," said Tom, as he took a bite of his sandwich and a gulp of beer.

"Isn't anyone suspicious that there may have been a major crime committed here?"

Tom swallowed.

"Yeah, I am."

"So, why did you, or anyone else, let this go through?" asked Trent accusingly.

"What could we do?" complained Tom. "There were lawyers involved. Everything was legal."

Trent narrowed his eyes in disgust at the banker.

"Well, finish your story. You say you've got a buyer, but she doesn't qualify. Who is she?"

The waitress came with two more beers, then left.

"She's the aunt of the husband of the couple killed in the car wreck. She's the one who should have had a chance to buy the place before Ben took over."

"Why doesn't she qualify?" asked Trent, who now began to eat his lunch.

"She might be able to make the payments, but she'd never have enough to pay off the back taxes and penalties," said Tom as he took a swig of beer.

Trent stopped eating and looked up.

"Back taxes? Penalties?"

"Yeah. Ben never paid a dime on real estate taxes since he owned the place."

"How did he get away with that?"

"He just didn't pay it, and the State of Alaska didn't seem to care. Now, it has to be paid at the time of the sale. I don't think this kid's aunt has that kind of money."

Trent looked at Tom for a moment to prepare himself for the answer to his next question.

"How much?"

"Uh, ten thousand plus change."

"Have you told her, yet?"

"No. She's coming up from Seattle and will be here tomorrow. She wants to look at the property."

Trent shook his head in disbelief. Could there be anyone as bad or evil as Ben. He didn't know it yet, but the answer was, yes.

Martha

"Trent!"

He was loading a box of traps into his plane when he heard Scotty call his name from in front of the pilot's lounge.

"Yeah?" he called back.

"Ya gotta visitor," hollered Scotty.

"Ya know," he said to Scotty on entering the door, "someday someone's gonna invent a phone you can carry around with you so we won't have to yell all the time."

"That'll be the day," laughed Scotty. "She's waiting for you in my office."

"She? What's she want? Who is she?"

"Go find out."

Trent entered the office and saw an attractive blonde woman, sitting on a chair. She looked to be in her forties, probably six to eight years younger than he, and wearing a beautiful fur parka.

She stood and smiled at him.

"Mr. Owen? I'm Martha Casey."

They shook hands.

"Please, sit down," he said as he took the swivel chair behind Scotty's desk. "How can I help you, Miss Casey?"

"Actually, it's Mrs. Casey," she said nervously, "but, please call me Martha."

"Okay, Martha, and you can call me Trent."

Martha's expression changed and Trent could tell she had some serious business.

"Tom Anderson, at the bank, told me you were interested in buying the Sky Harbor Hotel."

Trent smiled and shook his head.

"Not really. You must be the prospective buyer from Seattle?"

"Well, I was until I found out there was a lien against the place."

"He should have told you before you made the trip up here."

She looked saddened.

"My nephew and his wife owned it before this guy got his hands on it and wouldn't pay the taxes."

"You mean, Ben Barret?"

"You know, I believe he had something to do with my nephew's death."

Trent thought the same and wanted to help this woman.

"I believe he did too. But, he's dead now, and that's why the inn is up for sale again."

"Do you know what happened to him? I heard he disappeared and the inn reverted back to the bank because he wasn't making payments."

"He crashed on to a glacier. He's never coming back. He can't bother you."

She looked a little stunned, but relieved. Then she said, "So you have no interest in buying it?"

Trent thought a moment before he answered.

"I wouldn't know what to do with it. I'm a flyer and I've got my hands full running that business. I'm often gone for days at a time."

"But, if you had a good manager, you wouldn't have to be here."

That brought Trent up short.

"A good manager like whom?"

"Like me. I could run it. It was our dream to have an inn like this."

Trent reflected on the term, "our dream."

"Martha, are you divorced?"

Her expression saddened again.

"No. My husband was killed in Viet Nam."

Trent suddenly had a stabbing memory of his own wife's death.

"I'm sorry."

"I'm still trying to get over it," she said, as she produced a handkerchief and held it to her face. "He was a pilot too. He loved to fly. He was in the Air Force reserve and they called him back."

Trent couldn't resist asking the question.

"What happened?"

"He was an F-105 pilot. He was on a mission when he got hit from the ground. His wingman saw his plane go out of control and crash. He didn't get out of the plane, and it burned."

Then she burst into tears.

Trent went to her and held her while she cried. He was having the same old feelings about the loss of his wife, and tears trickled down his face.

There, the two once strangers held each other, and shared a common pain of loss.

A Close Call

"So, how are ya doing this, again?" asked Scotty, after he learned Trent was buying the inn with Martha.

"I put in the money to pay off the lien, and she's taking over the payments. Over time she'll buy my interest out, and then it's all hers," explained Trent.

"Well, that sounds like a good arrangement. She gets the hotel and you end up with a new girlfriend."

"C'mon, Scotty. It's strictly a business deal."

"Yeah, sure," laughed Scotty. "I'd like to be a fly on the wall when you two talk business."

"You're impossible," said Trent with a shrug. "Anyway, I'm expecting my fare anytime now," he said looking at his watch.

"Where ya goin'?"

"Up north on the coast. There's a polar bear hunter up there and I'm taking his son up to join him. I'll bet this is him coming now."

The door opened and a young Inuit man came into the pilot's lounge.

"Are you Trent?"

"Yeah. You must be James."

They shook hands.

"Which plane is yours?"

"The Cessna 185."

"I've got some provisions, a rifle and some ammo in my car. Can I drive up next to the plane and unload?"

"Sure."

150

Trent walked out to the plane while James got into his car and drove out to meet him. In a few minutes the plane was loaded, and James returned the car to the parking lot while Trent made some last minute checks on course headings and radio frequencies. Finally, James joined him and they began their flight.

"There's some bad weather ahead James. We might run into turbulence over some of those mountains. It's a long way out to the coast, so we'll have to refuel and spend the night in the village of Galina."

James nodded as if he understood. They climbed to nine thousand feet on a northwesterly heading. Trent kept in voice contact with the Anchorage Flight Center as he followed an invisible radio beam. The constant signal of dots and dashes, spelling, "ANC", in Morse code, let him know he was still on a narrow path extending from home. After a few hours he'd have to change frequencies, and pick up a new radial transmitted from Galina.

As they droned on, they became enveloped in clouds. Heavy snow streaked past the windows and beat on the windshield. James was frightened when he felt the plane lurch in all directions.

How can he stay on that tiny beam? he thought.

Then, he noticed the signal from Anchorage was getting weak and overcome with static. A violent updraft pushed him down in his seat, to be followed by a down draft that banged his head on the ceiling, even though he was belted in.

There was nothing to be seen through the windows. The clouds were no longer white, but turning gray, almost black. He could not hear the radio signal at all, and he watched Trent as he began turning dials.

"Galina control, this is Cessna 2446 Juliet, how do you read? Over."

Nothing but static.

"Galina, you read? Over."

Nothing.

James was beginning to get sick with the violent bucking of the plane, and now fear. He was sure something was wrong, but was afraid to ask.

Trent looked at his passenger and knew he must be frightened. He briefly put his hand on his shoulder, then back on the controls.

"James, we do have a problem. Galina's not answering. Their radio must be out."

"Can't we go back to Anchorage?"

"No. We're outta radio range, and low on fuel. We can't stay on this heading because of the mountains. I'm turning toward Galina based on where I think we are, and will keep trying to contact them."

James couldn't hold on any longer and vomited during the next updraft.

"Galina, this is Cessna 46 Juliet. We're low on fuel. Can you hear me?"

No answer.

"Why don't they answer?" asked James.

"I don't know. Maybe it has something to do with the military."

"Wadda you mean?"

"It's used as an auxiliary base by the Air Force. Maybe that has something to do with it."

He changed to the emergency frequency, 121.5 MHz.

"Galina, do you read?"

Suddenly, a voice boomed in the cabin. "Galina is closed."

"Look, we don't have much more than an hour of fuel left. We've got to land."

Silence.

"Did ya hear me?" he shouted.

"Make a ninety degree left turn. Don't acknowledge," came a response.

Immediately, Trent turned to the left, and tried to roll the unstable plane out at ninety degrees.

"What are they doin'?" asked a very sick and frightened James.

"Quiet!"

Then after what seemed like hours, "Return to your original heading."

Back again to the right, fighting to keep a constant altitude.

Again, silence.

Then, "Steer right ten degrees. I'll contact you later."

"What is it? What's goin' on?" cried out James, who now had vomited all over himself.

"I don't know," said a mystified Trent. "I think they're watching us on radar."

He didn't know whether he should change his altitude, or how far he was from the field. What if he had a headwind. His tanks might go dry before he got to where ever he was being sent.

Looking through the windshield that was being hammered by ice pellets and snow, they watched the daylight begin to fade into blackness. They continued on for nearly an hour. James began to reflect on his life, and pray.

"Lord, please help us. I'll quit swearing. I'll quit smoking. I'll go to church. I'll..."

"Say your altitude," boomed the speaker.

"Nine thousand feet."

"Let down to three thousand. Keep your course."

As they descended, they could see it brighten outside of the plane. The clouds around them became lighter. Finally at four thousand feet, they broke out of the overcast, and they saw a blacktop runway stretching out before them.

"You're clear to land."

Trent planted the wheels on the asphalt and let the plane roll to a stop, without touching his brakes. A jeep came down the runway from behind and passed them. They followed it off of the runway, and onto the taxi strip. As they headed for a group of buildings, they passed a row of F-106 delta wing fighter interceptors. Each plane had a pilot on board, with an electrical power unit attached. Milling about were several ground technicians.

"Wow!" said Trent. "Something is going on."

He parked the plane as directed, shut down the engine and got out, ready to face an agitated officer and his entourage awaiting him.

"What the hell were you doing out there?" demanded a colonel.

"We were on a flight plan from Anchorage," explained Trent, "and we couldn't raise the flight station here."

"We've got it shut down," said the colonel. "I'm sorry about that."

"What's goin' on?"

"Uh, we got a little war game goin' on with the Russians."

"For real?"

"I'm afraid so. Look, why don't you guys go with Sergeant Evans here. He'll take you to the mess hall and you can get something to eat."

Trent opened the baggage compartment of the plane and took out a pair of tie down bolts. He screwed them into the hard packed snow and attached them with ropes to the wing struts. They took out their overnight bags and followed the sergeant.

"Better take us to a latrine first, Sarge. I need to get cleaned up," said James.

Bait

After using a latrine and cleaning themselves up, they were directed by Sergeant Ron Evans to a barracks tent. There they put the bags they carried from the plane on to two empty cots that would be their's for the night.

James noticed mosquito netting over and around the tent. There were places in Alaska the mosquitoes were so thick one could inhale them. Galena was such a place.

"Does the netting do a good job keeping the mosquitoes out?" he asked.

"Well," replied the sergeant, "it works pretty good keepin' out the small ones, but the big ones just lift up the net and walk in."

Next the sergeant led them to the mess tent.

"Just grab one of those trays and go through the food line, then follow me to a table and have at it."

They each picked up a tray and utensils and followed their leader. The food line was set up cafeteria style. Several large serving pans were in a row on top of a long table. Behind each pan was a server manning a serving spoon. In each pan was a non-descript jumble of vegetables, meat and gravy.

"What is this stuff?" James asked the first server.

"C-Rations," replied the young man with a grin.

"Never thought I'd see them again," remarked Trent.

After loading up their trays, they sat down to a wooden table with bench seats.

After a few forkfulls, Trent noticed James was in to it.

"Not so bad after all, huh James?"

"Not when you're starving."

"I'm Ron Evans," said the sergeant.

"I'm Trent Owen and this is James," said Trent shaking his hand. Ron sat down across the table, facing them.

"I saw you guys come in with the Cessna. Are you a bush pilot?"

"I guess so," said Trent, trying to be modest.

"That's what I want to do when I get out of the Air Force in a few months."

"Oh?" said Trent. "You've got your licenses?"

"Yeah. I was flying before I went into the Air Force. I've got my commercial and instrument rating."

"Well, good luck to you," said Trent. "I hope you never have an experience like we did coming in here. What's going on?"

"I'm not supposed to say anything, but apparently the Soviets shot down a Navy P2V patrol plane near the Aleutians. They said it was in their airspace, but who knows where the boundary is when they're flying through storms and stuff."

"Where did you learn to fly, Ron?"

"In Tacoma, Washington. I worked at an airport there called, 'Tacoma Flying Service'."

"Really? That's where I learned to fly, back in the early fifties," said Trent. "What work did you do there?"

"I worked as a line-boy for a few years, while I was in high school. Part of my pay was in flight instruction."

"Did you know Leonard? He was the line-boy there when I was taking flying lessons."

"No kidding! The last I heard, he was flying for some company. Shell Oil, I think."

"Everett was my Instructor," said Trent. "Did you know him?"

Ron lowered his eyes and then looked up.

"Uh, Everett's dead."

"What!? What happened?"

"He was killed flying his brother-in-law's home built plane."

"I can't believe it. He was so experienced."

"They think there was some kind of structural failure. Anyway, he was too low when he bailed out. His chute never opened."

Trent shook his head with disbelief and sorrow.

Just then the colonel came up to them.

"Sergeant, could you please move to another table? I want a few words with our guests."

"Yes sir," said Ron and left.

"Colonel, I don't think we've been officially introduced. I'm Trent Owen, and this is my fare, James."

"I'm Colonel Bird. Pleased to meet you both," he said with a smile.

Trent put on a serious face.

"Colonel, do you know how close you came to killing us?"

The colonel's expression hardened.

"Let me tell you something. We are on the verge of an all-out war. The Russians shot down a Navy patrol plane yesterday, in our airspace in the Aleutians. This could be the beginning of the third world war, or it might have been a mistake. We don't know how our top brass is going to play it. But, if my superiors find out we broke radio silence from this base during a full scale alert, I'll be fried, and probably lose my commission."

"I'm sorry, Colonel. I'm also grateful you saved us. What do you want us to do?"

"Show me your destination," said the Colonel as he suddenly produced a chart.

Trent studied the map with James, and then pointed to an area that was really a drifting ice floe.

"Okay," said the Colonel. "Do you realize that chunk of ice has actually crossed the international dateline, and is now in Russian territory?"

"How would I know something like that?"

"Exactly! Tomorrow, I want you to continue your flight. What'll happen is, you'll pop up on the Russian radar and they'll send their interceptors to check you out."

"Oh. I see," said Trent. Then you guys will find out where their base is."

"Right."

"Why won't they kill us?"

"For one thing, you're a civilian so they wouldn't waste a rocket on you. And just think of the bad press they'll get around the world."

"What do you think, James? Should we do it?"

James shrugged.

"My dad needs the stuff we're hauling, and nothing could be as bad as we've just been through."

The next morning, before daylight, Trent and James had the plane fueled, and resumed their journey. Ron Evans was on duty at the time, and waved at them as they taxied past his airplane, on their way to the end of the runway.

They could see the F-106 fighters lined up and ready for war. The big delta winged jets were illuminated by portable lights, and surrounded by ground and flight crews. Each plane was armed with a rotary cannon.

"Man, these guys are really loaded for bear," quipped James.

"Yeah," said Trent. "Russian bear."

As instructed by Colonel Bird, they took off with no radio contact, and maintained an altitude of only five hundred feet above the ground. The rising sun gave promise of a clear but cold day.

James looked worried.

"How are we gonna find my dad?"

"Well," said Trent, "We're gonna stay on this heading for two hours. That'll bring us close to the Russian border, and near to where your dad should be. Then we'll climb to a high enough altitude to give us better visibility, and we shouldn't have trouble spotting a group of people on the white ice floe."

James sat quietly for a moment, looking at Trent.

"You sure the Russians won't shoot us down?"

"Colonel Bird didn't seem to think so," he said with a shrug.

"Don't ya think the Russians will know what we're doin'? I feel like a piece of bait, trying to catch a shark."

"Bear."
"What?"
"The Russians are bears, not sharks."
"I don't think this is funny," said James angrily. "I'm scared."
Trent looked at James, and gave him a wry smile.
"I'm scared too, but we're gonna do this."
They continued on their westerly course until Trent figured they were close to the border. He then climbed the Cessna to five thousand feet.
After about forty minutes, they saw a thin vapor trail high up in the dark blue sky, coming toward them from the southwest. Soon, a jet fighter plane took shape at the head of the trail, and made a large arcing turn, coming in behind the Cessna. The pilot lowered his landing gear and opened his speed brakes to slow down, but still flashed past.
"It's a MiG," shouted Trent to James.
The MiG fired a couple of red flares as he passed in front of the Cessna.
"What's he doin'!" cried James.
"He probably wants to talk to us, but I have no idea what frequency he's on."
"Why don't you use the same one you used to talk to Galina?" suggested James.
"Hey, good idea. I'll try the emergency channel."
Grabbing his mike, Trent tried to make contact.
"This is Cessna 2446 Juliet."
The response was in perfect English.
"You are in unauthorized airspace. What is your intention?"
"I'm taking a passenger and some supplies to a group of Inuits, who are hunting on an ice floe."
"You need to get permission to fly in Soviet airspace."
"We didn't know we'd be in your airspace," Trent lied. "The floe must have drifted."
The MiG was circling with about a two mile radius around them.
"You are very fortunate. We just settled the dispute we had with your country, otherwise you'd be dead right now."

Great! thought Trent. *I'll bet that colonel knew we'd be on a suicide mission.*

"I wouldn't have thought you'd waste a million dollar rocket on a small, defenseless civilian plane."

"I wouldn't have," said the MiG pilot. "I'd have used a 23 millimeter cannon shell. They're much cheaper."

Trent could feel the color drain from his face. James looked like he was about to vomit again.

"You're not far from the hunting party. Turn 20 degrees to your left and start descending."

Trent didn't say another word and followed the interceptor's instructions. Soon he spotted the hunters and set up for a landing on the floe. Once he was down, he taxied to the group and kept the engine idling. James opened his door and stepped out onto the Cessna's right ski.

"James, hurry up and get your stuff unloaded!" shouted Trent over the engine noise. "I'm really nervous about that MiG. He might suddenly get orders to blast my plane!"

After a few moments, James stepped away from the plane and gave Trent a wave.

Trent applied full power and lifted into the air. The MiG was still circling as he pointed the nose of the Cessna to the east, and headed back to Galina. He would have some choice words for Colonel Bird, if he was still there.

"Enjoy the rest of the day," said the MiG pilot as he disappeared into the dark blue depths of the sky.

Ron Evans

Flying with Moe

Ron Evans kept a terrible secret. He had killed a man.

It wasn't murder. He was not a murderer, but he intentionally killed a man. He did it in self-defense, but his problem was he had covered up the deed because he was afraid no one would believe him. With the passage of time, it was even more difficult to explain what had happened.

He was seventeen, still in high school, and had a private pilot's license. He worked as a line-boy for a flying school at a small airport in his hometown of Tacoma, Washington, and part of his pay was given to him as flying lessons. His popularity in school suddenly increased. He was no longer the shy, bespectacled gangly kid with few friends.

The airport was located in the northwest part of the city near the Tacoma Narrows, a fast flowing channel of Puget Sound. The water was spanned by a mile and a half long suspension bridge. The original bridge collapsed in a windstorm, only a few months after it's completion in 1940. A new bridge was built and opened in 1950. It was only six miles from the airport and became an important landmark for flyers, as it could be seen for miles around the Puget Sound area.

Ron's primary responsibilities as line-boy were to keep the planes refueled and tied down when they weren't used, and to start planes engines without a starter by "propping", or cranking the engine through compression by turning the propeller by hand. A dangerous thing to do, but, he was well trained.

There was a coffee shop on the airport where one could get a sandwich for lunch, or "hangar fly" with other pilots over a cup of coffee. The management had recently been taken over by an older couple, maybe in their sixties. The man's name was Moe. No one knew if "Moe" was the man's first or last name, so everyone referred to them as "Moe" and "Mrs. Moe".

Mrs. Moe did all of the work while her husband just hung around. She was a sweet Christian lady, and when she had a spare moment, she would read her Bible. She was very motherly and liked Ron. She would tell him about her church, and asked if he would go with her to the service sometime.

Moe didn't go to church. His Wife was so churchy, and he was just the opposite. He thought that he entertained everyone with his dirty jokes, dirty language and he was always puffing on a fat cigar, while his poor embarrassed wife was quietly fixing the food orders.

Ron didn't like the way Moe treated her. One day he walked into the coffee shop to grab a quick cup, and found Moe screaming at her. She was sitting at the counter crying with her head down in her arms. Ron didn't know what it was about, but it scared him and he turned around and left.

It became obvious something was wrong with Moe when one afternoon he showed up with an old bus, and parked it in the flying school parking lot. No one could figure out what he was going to do with it, especially Mrs. Moe who was beside herself.

"What did you do that for, Moe?" she moaned. "Why did you spend our money on an old bus?"

Ron didn't stick around long enough to finish his coffee, or to hear the answer, because he didn't like to see people upset, especially Mrs. Moe.

Moe became scarce around the coffee shop, showing up only once in a while in the afternoons. His wife would open the shop in the mornings, and then spend the whole day working alone. Often Ron and others would notice bruises and scratches on her face. Someone mentioned it looked like Moe was beating her up.

One Saturday afternoon, Ron noticed Moe standing outside of the coffee shop smoking. He looked at Ron and motioned him over to him. Ron walked up to him.

"Hey, kid! When you gonna give me that airplane ride you promised?"

He was right. Ron had promised to take him for a plane ride several weeks earlier when he just got his license.

"Uh, well I've been busy, Moe. I'll take you up sometime."

Moe wasn't going to be brushed off that easily.

"Look, kid, you promised."

Ron was a good kid, but he had a minor flaw. He was easily talked into things because he wanted to be liked by people, and he wanted to look good. He couldn't say, "no". It seemed a small thing, but it would be fatal.

The school's Cessna 140 was parked near by. Ron decided to use it, and pay off this perceived debt, once and for all.

"Okay, let's do it right now."

It was a two-place plane where the pilot and passenger would sit side-by-side. There are two sets of controls on all small planes, so an instructor can teach a student. Ron opened the right door and had Moe climb in. He then went around to the left side and got in. The engine was warm from a previous flight and started right up. It was a clear day, and the wind was coming from the north at about 15 to 20 MPH. They taxied to the south end of the runway, stopping short to check out the engine and controls, and then, continued to the center of the runway. Ron pushed the throttle to full open for take off.

The plane had just lifted off of the ground when suddenly Moe grabbed the control wheel.

"I can fly this fucking thing!" he slurred.

"Moe! What are you doing! Let go!"

In an instant Ron knew what Moe's problem was. Sitting close beside him he got a strong whiff of alcohol. The guy was stoned.

"Let go! Let go!" Ron yelled.

They were only about twenty feet in the air when they past over the end of the runway. Moe had a grin on his face and kept his grip.

At least the wings were level. Ron kept as much back pressure on the control wheel as he dared. He knew If Moe should suddenly let go of the wheel, the plane could go straight up, stall and fall on its back. The fuel tanks would break and they would probably burn to death

Gradually, Ron was getting the nose to a little higher attitude, and they slowly began to climb. He watched the altimeter slowly wind up. Eventually, they got up to 500 feet above the ground, and he felt he had a little more maneuvering room.

He kept pleading with Moe to let go, but he wouldn't. He just kept staring straight ahead, with an iron grip on the controls. A grip so tight in fact, when Ron tried to out muscle him on the control wheel he could feel the whole control column flex. He didn't know if it was possible to break anything, but sure didn't want to find out. He wasn't frightened at all, and his mind was racing trying to think what to do. He remembered in some movie he had seen where a student pilot froze on the controls, and the instructor knocked him out with a fire extinguisher. The only problem was there was no fire extinguisher in the plane.

Ron was making some progress by keeping back and left pressure on the controls, and pressing on the left rudder pedal. They were up to 800 feet now and they had made a wide 180-degree turn to the left, so they were now heading south. They were right over the middle of the Tacoma Narrows. The suspension bridge was just ahead of them, and they were going to cross over it at about mid span. Everything seemed surreal. Ron felt like he was outside of his body. It was like he was watching another person going through this struggle. He could hear himself yelling at Moe to let go, but it seemed like it was someone else.

What could he do? He thought about hitting him with his fist but quickly dropped that idea as he still had to hang on with both hands. Even if he did hit Moe, he could never put him out with just one punch, and then all hell would break loose.

They were at 1000 feet now and still heading south. They had just passed over the bridge and were still over the center of the channel. Now the plane began banking to the right. Ron resisted him as much as he dared, and kept enough pressure on the left rudder pedal to keep their heading generally to the south. He had to do something. How could he ever land the plane? Even if Moe did let go of the controls, what assurance did Ron have that he wouldn't grab them again during the landing approach when they would be close to the ground?

The plane was steeply banked and in a slip to the right, and they were losing altitude. Ron saw himself quickly take one hand off of the wheel, reach down and unsnap his own seat belt. Then he reached over and unsnapped Moe's belt and unlatched the passenger side door. Moe didn't seem to notice what Ron was doing. He still kept his grip on the wheel, and was in a trance. Even though the door was unlatched, it still looked closed because of the air pressure against it.

Everything seemed in slow motion and detached. Ron next saw himself turn in his seat and place his feet along the left side of Moe's body. With his back up against his own door, he pushed as hard as he could with his legs.

Most of Moe's body went out the right door, and he began to scream.

"No! No! Don't!"

There was no turning back now. Moe was still hanging on to the control wheel with his left hand. Ron reached over and pried his fingers loose from the wheel. Still screaming, he fell out some more and was now hanging onto the door opening. Ron stomped on his fingers with the heel of his shoe, and then he was gone

He quickly regained control of the plane and then looking though the side window, watched him fall to the waters below.

He watched as Moe's body fell in a graceful arc. He wondered why it wasn't in more of a straight line. It must have something to do with the relative motions that made it look like he was falling in a curve. Then, there was the splash. That took Ron out of his dream like state and he began to realize what happened. He could see something on the surface for a minute and then it disappeared.

He banked the plane to the left, and entered the airport traffic pattern on the downwind leg. He saw no other planes in the air. He pulled on the carburetor heat and throttled back as he turned onto base and then final approach. Landing a Cessna 140 can be a little tricky because the landing gear struts are spring steel, and tend to cause the plane to bounce. He bounced; partly because of the landing gear and partly because he was in such a hurry to get down. He taxied up to the gas pit and shut the engine down. The total flight only took ten minutes, but it seemed like a lifetime. What was going to happen to him? He felt terrible but couldn't see any other choice than what he made. Now, what should he do? Who would believe him?

He got out of the plane and could hardly stand. He had to steady himself by putting his hand out against the fuselage. After a while he regained his balance, and was able to refuel the plane. When he finished, he parked it on the flight-line and tied it down. He then walked over to the office and tried to ready himself for an explanation of a terrible event. Maybe he would end up going to prison.

He walked into the office ready to bare his soul. He thought he should tell his story to the airport owner.

"Bob, is Bud here?" he asked the office manager.

"No, he's not coming in today," he said as he sat at his desk shuffling papers. Then he looked up.

"Something I can help you with, Ron?"

"Uh, no. I just wanted to ask him something."

"He should be in tomorrow."

"I guess it'll keep," said Ron.

Bob returned to his papers, and Ron went back outside. It occurred to him no one noticed he had had even taken the plane. He didn't enter it on the schedule, and was only gone for ten minutes. He decided to say nothing.

He went about his work in a daze. He felt numb. Everything was in slow motion. He kept seeing Moe falling in that graceful curve to the water. At about four o'clock, Bob came out of the office and walked up to him while he was fueling a plane

"Ron, have you seen Moe today?"

He knew he would hear that question sometime soon

"No! Why?"

"His wife's looking for him. She says he was here earlier, but then he just disappeared."

"Did she think I'd know where he was?"

"She didn't ask me to ask you, I just thought you might have seen him."

"Nope!"

Bob walked back toward the office. Ron stayed away from the coffee shop.

The next morning Mrs. Moe didn't come in to open up the coffee shop. The airport staff wasn't going to spend a day without caffeine, so someone used a spare key from the office and all had free coffee. The day went pretty much as usual. He didn't hear anyone mention a thing about Moe. No one else seemed to be thinking about him. He couldn't get the picture out of his mind of Moe's body falling in that long slow motion arc to the water. He would never forget it.

Later on in the afternoon, Bud called everyone into the office. When Ron walked in, all of the mechanics, instructors and office staff were there along with a few students, who were in the office at the time. There was also a man there Ron had never seen before, and he was standing next to Bud. After the buzz of people talking quieted down, Bud spoke up and introduced the man.

"Everyone! This is Officer Cameron from the Tacoma Police Department. He wants to ask us some questions about what's happened to Moe."

"Hi!"

He paused for a minute and then asked, "Is there anyone here who saw Mr. Moe at anytime yesterday?"

No one spoke up.

"His wife said he came to the coffee shop about two o'clock yesterday. The last she saw him was when he stepped outside to smoke."

Bud looked at Ron.

"Ron, you're outside most of the time. Did you see him?"

He felt his face burning. He wondered if policemen could just look at you and tell you were guilty, or if you were lying.

"No."

Cameron was looking at him now too. He wondered if he answered too quickly. Maybe his voice was too high pitched out of fear.

"What do you do here?" he asked Ron.

"I gas airplanes," he said.

Bud explained to the detective that Ron was the line-boy, and that he worked after school during the week and all day during the weekends.

Then Cameron addressed everyone.

"We know he was probably here. He took the bus from downtown because his wife had the car. He doesn't drive anyway, because his license was taken from him for driving drunk. I talked with the bus driver and he remembered him because he got off at the end of the line, which is here at the airport. His wife said she saw him for only a few minutes, and then he disappeared. And none of you saw him?"

Everyone either shrugged their shoulders, or shook their head, or said no.

Cameron thanked everyone for their time and left. All went back to what they were doing.

The next day, Ron saw Moe's wife was back, and the coffee shop was open. He kept busy and tried not to think about what had happened. Then it occurred to him he should go into the coffee shop during his break. Maybe it would look suspicious if he stayed away.

He went there on his break, and Mrs. Moe poured him a cup. He sat there sipping it. He was there alone with Mrs. Moe. He was just about to tell her about how sorry he was her husband was missing when Officer Cameron walked in.

The officer remembered him said, "Ron, is Bud here?"

I think so.

"Would you find him and tell him I'll come over to the office in a few minutes? I want to talk with him."

"Sure!" said Ron and then went out the door.

He found Bud in his inner office talking to someone on the phone. He stood there in the doorway, making sure he was noticed. In a minute or so Bud hung up the phone and gave Ron his attention.

"That policeman is back again and he wants to talk with you."

"Where is he now?"

"Over at the coffee shop talking to Moe's wife!"

"Huh! He must have some news."

The only ones now left in the office was an instructor with his student, Chuck, the office manager, Bud, and himself. In a little while Cameron came into the office.

"Hi!" Bud greeted him.

"Hi, Bud! Well I've got some news about Mr. Moe!"

Everyone was now ready to hear what he was about to say, especially Ron. Again he wondered if someone saw him get into the plane with Moe, or if someone saw him fall.

Officer Cameron went on.

"His body was found on the beach at McNeil Island."

The Federal Government owns all of McNeil Island where there is a big penitentiary. The only people allowed there are the inmates and workers who live there.

"It seems that some of the kids who live there found him. The Coast Guard picked up his body and brought it to Tacoma. It was pretty badly damaged. Even one of his shoes was torn off. We think he had to fall from a pretty good height to cause the damage. I think he must have jumped from the Narrows Bridge, which is probably high enough."

Everyone there was nodding their heads in agreement with findings and assumptions.

Cameron went on, "The only thing I can't figure is how he got to the bridge from here? He didn't drive because his wife still has the car. There's no bus service between here and the bridge."

Ron was eager to suggest a theory and said, "Maybe he hitched a ride."

Cameron thought about that for a second or two and then said, "No! I don't think so. If he was as drunk as the bus driver says, I don't think anyone would pick him up."

Ron wondered why he didn't know he was drunk. He didn't seem to stagger when he saw him. Why didn't he smell the alcohol on his breath right away?

So Officer Cameron ended with his conclusion. Moe had jumped off of the bridge. But how he ever got to the bridge was, and would always be a mystery.

Gradually, everything became normal again and over the years, memories dimmed. Ron went on to earn his Commercial Pilot's license and later join the Air Force. He wondered how Mrs. Moe's life had turned out. He wondered if she became happier, or if she actually missed her husband.

Flight to Anvik

"Fairbanks Center, Cessna 84 Kilo, has Anvik in sight."
"Roger, 84 Kilo. Are you planning to return to Fairbanks today?"
"Affirmative. I can't think of a single reason to stay here."
"I've heard Eskimos share their wives with visitors," joked the controller.
Ron laughed. "No, I think they all sleep in the same bed to keep from freezing. That's what my wife told me, and she's an Inuit."
"Now I know," said the controller. "Anyway, I'll keep your flight plan open for your return. Just give me a holler when you're back in the air."
"Thanks."
Ron landed on the airstrip marked by an outline of brush and debris. As he taxied to some out buildings, children came running out of their homes, and on to the runway. He had to stop a moment for fear one would run into the prop. They can't see it when it's turning. It's a tragedy that's happened more than once. Some adults appeared, and chased the kids out of the way.
He stopped the plane near a group of people, shut down the engine and opened the door.
"Greetings," he said.
One of the men came to the door.
"You must be Ron," he said. "I'm Hugo."
"Glad to meet you, Hugo. I've got a bunch of traps for you."
"You look so young. Do you know how to fly?"

"Well, I got here, didn't I?" smiled Ron, as he stepped down from the plane, and opened the baggage compartment.

"How old are you?" Hugo persisted.

"I'm 24 and you haven't seen me before, 'cause I just got out of the Air Force and I'm new at this. I'll let you guys take these traps out of the plane. I don't want one clamping on to my hand."

"They're not triggered. They won't hurt you," said Hugo, as he and a couple of other men started pulling them out of the plane.

"Yeah? I've heard that same story about the unloaded gun shooting someone. Now, the broker told me you have some pelts for me to take back."

"Yes," said Hugo.

Some of the women pulled up a sled, piled high with all kinds of furs. Ron could see skins from otters, seals, wolves and even a couple of polar bears.

"Whoa! I can't take all these."

The Cessna 180 is a great bush plane. It has a good cruising speed and it's a heavy lifter, but like any other plane, it had a load limit.

"Take what you can. Other pilots have taken this much."

Ron doubted that, and thought Hugo was just trying to convince him to take the whole load. But, how could he know for sure without scales.

"They don't weigh much," continued Hugo. "It's just the pelts. Let's see how many we can get in."

Ron was stymied. He just stood there and watched as they crammed every pelt in to the baggage hold.

"See? We got it in. They fit. You gotta big plane. You'll be able to take-off."

"So, what am I supposed to do when I get to Fairbanks?" Ron asked.

"See The Fur Traders Company. They're the ones who sent you here. They'll take the pelts from you, and put money into our village account. It works just like a bank. The money belongs to the village, and is distributed to our families."

"Wow! What a deal," said Ron. "Well, I'd better leave while there's some daylight."

He shook hands with Hugo, waved good-by to the others, mounted his plane and taxied to the end of the airstrip. After checking out the engine, he lined up on the runway. He set his flaps for take-off, and pushed the throttle all the way forward.

At the halfway point down the runway he tried to lift the plane, but it wouldn't budge. At three quarters of the way, the skis were still stuck to the ground. Now he knew he should never have let Hugo talk him into taking the full load.

At the last moment, with the end of the runway staring him in the face, he grabbed the flap handle and gave a quick jerk. The plane leaped in to the air, and then started settling back down. He managed to hold it only inches above the terrain while slowly building up airspeed. Gradually, the plane began to climb. He was thankful there were no obstructions off the end of the airstrip.

After he caught his breath, he reached for the microphone.

"Fairbanks Center, this is Cessna 84 Kilo, on the return flight."

"Roger, 84 Kilo. Say your altitude."

"Three thousand."

"Roger, Kilo. We'll expect you back in about an hour and a half."

As he settled into his flight, he could feel the deceiving rays of the warm afternoon sun. Even though the calendar said it was early spring, the nights were well below zero, especially during the clear weather. The cool temperatures were good for flying as the air is denser and more efficient for both the engine and the wings of his plane.

He had earned his commercial pilot's license at the age of eighteen, and then joined the Air Force. He started his flying career soon after he was discharged from Ladd Air Force Base near Fairbanks, and now became a freelance flyer.

He began to dream how his new business would someday provide a good living for him and Sharon. He actually met her in a bar. He was lonely, and she was a good companion. Fortunately, she wasn't hooked on drugs or alcohol, and she gave a woman's touch to his home. His friends teased him, and referred to her as "Ron's Klooch," a highly derogatory word for an Inuit or Eskimo woman. He made it clear to them he had feelings for her, and they stopped the insults.

Ron and Sharon had no intentions of marrying, or having children. She had someone to take care of her, and he had someone to come home to and love.

They lived in a small house a few miles outside of the town of Delta Junction, where the Alcan and Richardson Highways joined. Ron got his plane by taking over the payments from the previous owner, who had left the area. He could keep the Cessna next to his house during the winter months, when everything was covered with snow and ice. In the summer months, or during the thaw, he would have to move the plane to the town airport and replace the skis with wheels. The fuel and maintenance costs tended to keep him broke.

Now, he was on his way to Fairbanks where he would refuel, and spend the night. He was tired, and was daydreaming about the Polaris Hotel, where he looked forward to dinner and…"

"Whoa! What's that?" he said aloud, as he spotted something on the ground. He put the plane in a circle to the left so he could get another look. Coming around again he could see a small snow covered mound with an opening on the side of it. Grabbing his binoculars he could see it was a bear's hibernation den, and the snow around it had not been disturbed.

"Huh! I'll bet there's a grizzly in there," he said to himself. "He's probably still hibernating."

As he circled he moved the pitch control lever forward, causing the propeller to make a loud rapping sound. He watched the den opening to see if the noise would drive the animal out, but there was no movement. The undisturbed snows told him the bear was still in his den, and probably sound asleep.

He went back to his course to Phelps Field at Fairbanks. About an hour later he picked up his radio mike.

"Fairbanks Center, this is Cessna 84 Kilo."

"Go ahead, Kilo."

"I've got Phelps in sight. Please close my flight plan."

"Roger, Kilo. Good day."

"Thanks."

Ron landed and was met by a man from the furrier company.

"Wow. I think you've got the biggest load I've seen from a plane this size."

Ron shook his head as he helped transfer the pelts from the plane to the man's truck.

"Too big of a load. I almost didn't get off the ground. It won't happen again."

After the man drove away, he made his refueling and tie-down arrangements with Franklin, the field owner and operator, and then found a ride going into town. He walked into the Polaris Hotel, and stepped up to the desk.

"Hi, Sally."

"Hi, Ron. I suppose you want a room."

"Yeah. Give me something cheap."

After registering, he went to the room, threw his overnight bag on to a chair, and flopped on the bed.

Seduction

Ron slept for two hours, and when he opened his eyes again, it was seven o'clock PM. He was hungry, and thirsty for a cold beer. He got to his feet, stretched, and then left his room. He took the elevator down to the lobby, and walked into the lounge and sat down at the bar. Charlie, the bartender, was talking with a fellow who was sitting on the next stool, and they were looking at an album of pictures. Ron caught Charlie's eye.

"Hello, Ron. What can I get you?" asked Charlie.

"How about a glass of amber ale and an order of nachos?"

"You've got it," said Charlie as he wrote down the order.

Ron glanced at the man sitting next to him, who had been talking with Charlie. He looked to be about forty, wore a tweed coat and a tan shirt, open at the collar. He turned and looked at Ron.

"How ya doin'?" said the man

Ron was surprised at the man's familiarity.

"Okay."

The man seemed drunk because he was slurring his words.

Maybe it was an accent. He's probably from the states, Ron thought. *Maybe up here on business and just wants to talk.*

"Do ya live up here?" asked the man.

"Well, I live in Delta Junction. It's a town between here and Anchorage."

"What kind of work do ya do?"

Ron liked to tell people about his work. He was always a little shy and self conscious, but, when he talked about his flying, he felt people became interested and respected him. It was a crutch for his lack of social skills.

"I'm a pilot."

"A what?"

"You know. A flier."

"Ya mean ya work for an airline?"

"No. I'm a bush pilot."

"Wow! No kiddin'?"

A waitress behind the bar appeared in front of Ron with his order of nachos and a glass of beer.

"Here ya go. Enjoy," she said.

"Thanks."

The man grinned at Ron, and then introduced himself.

"My name's Johnny. Johnny D'Angelo."

"I'm Ron Evans."

"You like beer?"

"Cheaper than anything else."

Johnny called to the bartender. "Hey, Chucky, or Charlie, or whatever your name is, gimme two shots of bourbon."

Charlie set up two shot glasses in front of Johnny and filled them. Johnny pushed one over to Ron and said, "Here."

"Ah, well, I got a beer right now."

"No problem."

Johnny picked up the shot glass and poured into Ron's beer glass.

"Now ya gotta souped up beer," Johnny said with a grin.

"Well, thank you."

The man was being nice. Maybe a little assertive, but Ron didn't see any reason to be wary of him. Not yet anyway.

"Let's sit over at one of da tables where it's quieter," said Johnny. "I wanna hear more about your job. Sounds exciting."

Johnny picked up his picture album, and Ron followed obediently with his chips and drink.

"Two more drinks!" Johnny called to the bartender. Then he focused on Ron.

"So how long have you been doing dis bush flyin'?"

"I'm just starting."

"What is it ya do when ya fly?"

While Ron thought for an answer, a girl brought over the drinks. He felt a little elated. Someone was showing interest in him, and buying drinks, and wants to hear about what he does.

"Well, I'm probably like a cab driver."

"A cab driver?"

"Yeah. People hire me to take them somewhere."

"What people?"

"Oh, could be hunters, or prospectors, or even missionaries."

"Missionaries? You fly missionaries around?"

More drinks came.

"So what do you do, Mr. Ah...?"

"Johnny. Just call me Johnny. Right now I'm a trophy hunter. I used to be a boxer a few years back, but I'm too old now."

"What's a trophy hunter?"

"It's someone who bags special animals."

"You mean like lions or tigers?"

"Sort of."

"Is that what you got in your album? Pictures of your trophies?"

"Yeah. Would ya like ta see some?"

"Sure."

Johnny slid the album across the table between the two of them and opened it. Each page of the album was a plastic envelope containing an eight and a half by eleven photograph. The first picture was of a lion. It looked like it was leaping right out of the page.

"Wow! That's good," said Ron. He saw in the other pictures the animals were very close and were either leaping or charging.

"Man!"

"Pretty good pictures aren't dey?"

"I'll say."

More drinks came.

"Here's a picture of a charging elephant," said Ron. "I thought it was illegal to hunt elephants."

"Well, some places have these silly laws on their books. As long as you don't bring the animal out of the bush, how will anyone know?"

Ron felt puzzled.

"How do you collect the trophies if you leave them there?"

"Dat's what the photos are for."

"Yeah, but to kill an animal just for a picture?"

"Animals die all da time. Just because you shoot one isn't gonna change the worl', is it?"

"No. Probably not," said Ron, feeling something wasn't right.

"If you're running a taxi service, maybe you could help me. I need a grizzly bear for my collection. Maybe we could go up in your plane and look for one."

"I already know where there's one," Ron said before he could stop himself.

"Ya do? Where?"

"About a hundred miles from here."

"Really? Did ya see it?"

"No. I saw the opening to its den."

"It's still hibernatin'. That'll be easy."

"But we can't do that. It's not hunting season. You can't even get a permit."

"Can ya show me on a map where you saw dis den?"

"I have my charts in my room."

"I'll order another round while you get dem."

Ron dutifully got up and went to his room.

"Why am I doing this?" he mumbled. He was feeling trapped.

When he came back to the bar Johnny was waiting for him. They spread the chart out on the table and Ron pointed to the spot.

"Right there."

"Will you take me there?"

"No! I don't want to get into trouble."

"Look. Ya don't have a t'ing ta worry about. I'm da hunter. All you're gonna do is take a picture."

Ron was about to protest again, when Johnny said, "There's five thou' in it for you. If you like, I'll write the check right now."

Five thousand dollars! Ron thought. *That would pay a few bills.*

Johnny pulled out a checkbook from his coat pocket and started writing.

Morning

    Ron had his home in sight. He throttled back, lowered the flaps and plunked down on the snow. The plane slid right up to the back of his house. He climbed out, and opened the door to his kitchen. There was Sharon, waiting for him. He closed the door behind him, and they fell into an embrace. The five thousand dollar check was in his hand.
    "Look! Look what I've got!"
    Then, there was a noise at the door. Bang! Bang! Bang!
    "What's that?"
    "No! No! Don't open it!" Sharon cried as he left her and went to the door. "It's a bear!" she cried. "Don't open it!"
    Bang! Bang! Bang!
    The noise was giving him a headache.
    Bang! Bang! Bang!
    Ron opened his eyes. Gradually, his hotel room came into focus. The clock on the nightstand showed nine o'clock.
    Is it morning or night? he wondered.
    Bang! Bang! Bang! Came the pounding from the door. His head ached.
    "Who is it?" he called.
    "Hey! It's me! Johnny! Lemme in."
    Ron got out of bed and opened the door, and there stood Johnny in a camouflage hunting outfit, including a parka and rubberized boots.

"You look a little hung over, Ron. Are you gonna be okay?"

"Sure."

"Look, why don't ya' take a shower, have breakfast and coffee, and when you feel better come get me? I'm in 726."

"Sure."

Johnny turned to leave, and Ron closed the door.

Now, he remembered everything that happened last night, up to the point when Johnny handed him the check. After that it was just bits and pieces. He pulled on his pants and checked his pockets. Everything was there, including the check from Johnny. At least he hadn't dreamed that.

Thinking about dreaming, he shuddered at remembering the dream he just had. It was such a warm and wonderful dream, about coming home, about Sharon, and about five thousand dollars. Then there was the pounding at the door. Sharon became frightened and said it was a bear. He went to the door. He had the choice of opening it or not. Then he woke up, and opened the door to his room.

Was it the money that snared him? Or, was it the powerful influence that Johnny had over him. He remembered what someone told him once. Evil recruits its victims.

After he finished dressing, he left the hotel and had breakfast at a diner down the street. His headache was gone, and he was feeling much more alive. After his meal, he went to the bank and deposited the check into his account. It was a joint account he shared with Sharon. He was the only one who made transactions, but he wanted it to be available to her in case something ever happened to him.

He returned to the hotel, and went up to his room on the fourth floor. Stepping out of the elevator he saw Johnny in the hallway.

"Feeling better?" asked Johnny.

"Yeah. Are you ready to go?" Ron asked, as he entered his room.

"I can hardly wait," said Johnny.

Ron stuffed the Alaska sectional chart back into his map case.

"Have you called a cab to take us to the airport?" asked Ron.

"Don't need to. I've got a rental car. Say, don't ya need some heavier clothes?" said Johnny, after noticing Ron was only wearing denim pants, shirt and jacket.

"All my cold weather gear is in the plane," said Ron. "And I am wearing my rubberized boots because of all of the thawing."

They went down to the lobby and to the desk.

"May I help you?" asked a young man.

"We're going to be gone, and if we're not back by this evening, we should be back here tomorrow morning," Ron told the desk man.

"Okay. Please leave your keys, and pick them up when you come in."

They handed over their keys, and walked out the door.

As Johnny drove the car, Ron was quiet and deep in thought. He wished he hadn't gotten himself into this situation. It was the easy money that caused him to become involved.

"Did ya have any trouble cashing da check?" Johnny asked.

"What?"

"Da check was good, wasn't it?"

"Yeah."

They were both quiet for a while. Then Ron looked at him and said, "You were a prize fighter?"

"Yeah. I was."

"Were you good?"

"I almos' became the Middleweight Champion."

"You must have made a lot of money."

Johnny laughed, "I made more money losing a bout den winning."

"You'd make money for losing?"

"Dat and other t'ings. Normally I don't tell people about my business. But, you're an exception. I don't see how anyt'ing you could do would have any effect on me."

"How did you profit from killing animals?" asked Ron.

"Two ways. I got da pictures I wanted, den we'd sell da bush meat."

"Bush meat?"

"Yeah. Da African natives developed a taste for wild animals. Dey crave it. Dey call it bush meat and dey pay big money fer it. Dere favorite was apes and gorillas."

Ron was totally disgusted, and he didn't like Johnny at all.

"I don't want to do this."

"Why? What's the matter? You got an attack of conscience?"

"Normally, I'd never do something like this."

"Unless you got paid for it. Everyone's got a price. Yours was five grand. The people I worked for have always kept me in money. You don't make money obeying da law. You make money by breaking da law. A lot of money."

"You can do these things without even feeling guilty?" asked Ron.

"Not a twinge. Now, why don't ya quit whining and enjoy da day?"

They reached the airport and parked the car. Johnny opened the trunk and pulled out his rifle scabbard.

"I have to settle with Franklin," said Ron.

"Go ahead. I'll wait at da plane."

"Where ya headed, Ron?" asked Franklin, as he wrote out a receipt for gas and tie down.

"I'm taking this guy on a scenic flight."

"It looks like he's carrying a rifle."

"Uh, he says it's expensive. He doesn't want it out of his sight."

"Are you filing a flight plan?"

"No, we'll just be local. I won't need one."

Franklin looked at Ron over the top of his glasses.

"Well, what ever you say," said Franklin as he took the money and handed over Ron's receipt.

"Why don't you keep that thing outta sight," Ron said to Johnny as he approached the plane.

He took the rifle that was leaning against the fuselage and shoved it into the baggage compartment.

Johnny laughed at him. "You're sure nervous."

"I've got reasons to be nervous. I feel like everything I'm doing is wrong."

Ron closed up the compartment. Johnny took his camera out of its case.

"Hey, Ron. I wanna take your picture before we leave. Stand next to da plane."

Ron stood next to the front of the plane, and posed with his left hand resting on a propeller blade, until he heard the camera "click." Then a thought flashed through his mind about Sharon. She never wanted to have her picture taken because one of her tribal superstitions was the camera captured the soul.

They climbed into the plane and started up. Ron checked out the engine as they taxied to the end of the runway. Satisfied everything was in the "green" and there was no traffic, he line up on the runway, and took off.

Immediately he steered on to course as they were still climbing. Flying without a flight plan was a risk, but he didn't want anyone to know where he was going.

"I've never been up in a small plane before," said Johnny. "Dis is beautiful."

It was a glorious day. Just like many of them. Nothing but sunshine and blue sky. The ground was a carpet of white, and the surrounding mountains glistened with reflected light.

Johnny was impressed. "Is learning ta fly a hard t'ing ta do?" he asked Ron.

"To some people."

"Do ya t'ink I could learn ta fly?"

"I don't know."

"Hey! What's dose animals down dare?"

"Caribou."

"Dere're so many of 'em."

"They hang out in herds. You know, that would be an easy trophy for you. Sometimes they're right next to a road. You could shoot one without even getting out of your car."

"I don't t'ink dey're on my list," said Johnny.

He then leaned back in his seat, and watched the scenery as it rolled by.

Den

After an hour's flight, they came up on a frozen lake large enough for them to land, Ron reduced power and began to let down for a straight in approach.

"Is dis da place?" asked Johnny.

"It's just beyond the far shore."

The lake was about three miles in diameter, giving plenty of room for landing and take-off. When the skis made contact with the snow, he used enough power to reach a little beyond the shore where they stopped.

"Wow! Dat was neat!" crowed Johnny as he climbed down from the plane.

Ron opened the baggage compartment and pulled out his parka. The same one issued to him by the Air Force. He tested the snow crust and decided they wouldn't need snow shoes.

Johnny pulled out his rifle scabbard and opened it, exposing a beautiful instrument.

"Is that new?" asked Ron.

"No. Me an' dis rifle go way back."

"This is what you used for poaching?"

"If dat's what ya call it. You don't know nothing about me," Johnny said with a wicked smile. "Killin' the animals was only part of da fun."

"Wha'd you mean?"

"Another guy and me ran a safari business in Tanzania. We'd get rich people from all over da worl' dat would sign up for one of our trips."

"To shoot protected animals?"

"Dat was only part of da gig," said Johnny, smiling to himself, as he reminisced. "Now, we couldn't let anyone report on what we were doin', could we?"

"You killed the porters!"

"After we were finished wit' dem. Dey were more fun to hunt den da animals."

"Why?" cried Ron. "Why would you do a thing like that?"

Johnny broke out in laughter.

"What's so funny?"

"Here's da funny part. We'd get rid of dere bodies da same way we got rid of da animals. Bush meat! Ain't dat a kick?"

Ron detested him. This guy was pure evil and he didn't know how to get away from him.

"How could you even consider doing something like that?"

"Why not? Dey're just like any other animal. Dey live for a while, and den die. Besides, what good are dey? Dey're just natives. Dey don't do nuthin'. Dey don't read or write. Dey don't work. Dey don't…"

"You arrogant bastard! I can't believe people like you exist."

"Well, ya asked, and right now yer lucky I can't fly a plane," Johnny said as he leveled the weapon at Ron's chest. Then he grinned. "Don't worry, I haven't loaded it yet." He then propped it up against the side of the plane.

Ron could feel his face burn, but wisely decided not to escalate hostilities.

"So where do we go from here?" asked Johnny.

"The den is only a mile away. We go up over that draw, then there's a ridge."

"Lead da way."

It took twenty minutes to walk into the small flat valley where Ron had seen the den from his plane. Johnny was out of shape, and was sweating badly from the exertion, and from wearing too many warm clothes.

"Is dat where da den is?" asked Johnny, pointing to a slight mound about a hundred yards in front of them.

"I think so."

He fished some shells out of his pocket and began to load his rifle.

"How come you're loading so many shells, Mr. One Shot?" asked Ron. He couldn't resist the barb, but Johnny just ignored him.

They began walking slowly toward the den. Soon they could see the opening. It looked small because snow above it collapsed and partially filled it in. They stopped their advance about fifty feet from the opening. Johnny removed the camera strap from around his neck and gave it to Ron, who was right behind him.

"Here. All ya have ta do is point and shoot. It's already ta go. I want ya ta snap the picture as soon as I fire."

Ron took the camera, and looped the strap around his neck. They again started slowly walking forward in a crouch. Johnny chambered a round in his rifle, and held it in a ready position.

"I don't think he's asleep. There are foot prints around the den," said Ron. "The breeze is at our backs. He knows we're here."

Now, they stopped just a few feet in front of the opening. Johnny looked back at Ron.

"Get dat camera ready."

Suddenly, a brown explosion burst out of the opening.

Discovery

A Glint of Silver

"I'd hate to lose an engine about now, Doc", said Trent Owen, as he looked down on the mountainous terrain.

He and Doc Watson were northwest of Anchorage, on a flight to the Eskimo coastal village of Shishmar.

"You didn't have to say anything," said Doc. "I hate flying."

Trent had a contract with the missionary couple, Rod and Jenny Ames, who were living there. The village was about two hundred miles southwest of Fairbanks. Every two weeks, weather permitting, he'd bring in supplies, and take out a load of pelts. This time Doc came with him, to check on Jenny, who was now pregnant.

"The weather's perfect, except for the ground fog."

"Yeah, but it's not like the ice fog that forms in the winter," said Doc. "That's when you can frostbite your lungs in a heartbeat."

They'd been in the air over two and a half hours above a mountainous wilderness that stretched in all directions.

"Hey, what's that over there?" said Doc.

Trent saw a glint of silver from the ground. He put the Cessna 185 into a circle around an object reflecting sunlight through a thin sheet of fog.

"It looks like it might be a plane on the ground," said Trent as he reached for his radio mike.

"Anchorage Center, this is Cessna 2446 Juliet."

"Go ahead, 46 Juliet."

"Do you know of any missing planes?"

"Haven't heard of anything. What've ya got?"

"I saw a shiny refection through the ground fog, but I can't see it now."

"We show you on our radar to be about 270 miles on the 310 radial from Anchorage. Are you gonna land and check it out?"

"Negative. I gotta make my delivery. I'm planning to refuel in Fairbanks this afternoon, and spend the night. I'll look again on my way back tomorrow."

"OK 46 Juliet. Enjoy your flight."

Trent took a pencil and marked his sectional chart as best he could. The fog was obscuring land marks, but he'd flown the route many times and felt confident he was close. He went back to his original heading, and wondered about what he had seen. There was little question in his mind it was a plane, but was it an intentional landing, or something else.

The Village of Shishmar

They continued on their way to the tiny village, and landed the ski equipped plane in a small cleared off area.

Before Trent could shut the engine down, the plane was surrounded by kids. He worried someday one would get killed. Some of the adults were just as bad. When they climbed down out of the plane, Jenny came up to greet them.

"Hi, Trent. How are you?"

"Hi, Jenny," he responded as she gave him a hug.

"Hey, don't I rate one of those too?" said Doc.

"Of course," said Jenny. "Welcome to our village," she said as she hugged Doc.

Rod and Jenny Ames were Presbyterian missionaries, and have been living in the village for the past three years. Rod, an ordained pastor, preached on Sundays and, with Jenny, would help the village members with alcohol addiction, and domestic abuse programs. They were in their early thirties, and were truly loved by the people they served.

"What did you bring me?" she asked.

"Well, you got a bunch of mail, and some groceries. Salt, sugar, flower, oil, eggs, coffee, milk. You won't have to eat blubber for a while."

They all laughed.

"Where's Rod?" Trent asked.

"He's helping one of the teenagers repair his snowmobile."

"The kids have snowmobiles now? I thought these people were poor."

"Snowmobiles are important. They need them for hunting polar bear and seals. They buy cheap used ones, and the bank in Anchorage helps them with a loan."

The village kids unloaded the plane, and were carrying the stuff, as they all walked to Jenny's house.

"Hey Jenny, your looking a lot bigger," said Doc. "I'd say you're due in about three more months."

"You be sure to give me plenty of time to come and get you," said Trent. "I can't help you and fly at the same time, if you decide to have the baby in the plane."

"Maybe I'll use the village midwife."

"I don't think that's a good idea," said Doc.

They reached her house, or more aptly, "shack." No one in the village knew how old it was. It was made with a single layer of clapboard siding, and no insulation. The inside was divided into a kitchen, a living room and a bedroom. In the middle of the living room was a stove made from a 55 gallon oil drum. There was no shortage of blubber or seal oil, which was used to burn and give off heat. Trent could never figure out how it was done.

Electricity was available from diesel generators. The fuel was brought in overland by tanker trucks during the summer months, and kept in huge storage tanks. Each home had a hotplate and microwave for cooking, and a television set. The entire village shared a common antenna, high up on a tower, on the highest point near-by. The signal was dispersed by cables to each home. Reception was fair from one, and sometimes two stations. Trent and Doc hadn't eaten anything since they left Anchorage, and were hungry. Jenny was putting away groceries the neighbor kids carried in from the plane, when Rod came in the door ready for lunch.

"Hi, Trent, Doc. Good to see you."

They shook hands as they greeted each other.

"Hey, I know you guys are hungry," said Jenny. "I'll heat up some stew, and let's have some lunch."

"Sounds good to me," said Trent.

They sat down at the table, and Rod asked a blessing. Then they ate and talked.

The stew had pieces of unidentified meat floating in it. Doc stabbed one of the pieces with his fork and put it in his mouth. He chewed and chewed but couldn't break it down enough to risk swallowing. In fact, the piece seemed to be increasing in size. He looked over at Trent, who also seemed to be having trouble swallowing his chunk. He worked his mouthful into one cheek so he could talk.

"Uh, Jenny, what kind of stew are we eating?"

"Do you like it?" she said with a smile.

"Yeah, but, it seems kind of 'gummy'."

"When we're finished with lunch, I'll tell you what it is."

Trent and Doc looked at each other, and then said in one voice, "It's not dog, is it?"

Both Rod and Jenny laughed.

"No, it's not dog. Take smaller bites and it'll be easier to chew."

Finally, the two visitors got in control of their stew enough so they could talk.

"So are you guys ready for your first kid?" asked Doc.

"Do we have a choice?" laughed Rod.

"Well, what's one more?" said Doc. "Seems to me you already have a family of village kids running through your house."

"They don't have any sense of personal property," said Rod. "We just get used to it."

"So, what's going on with you, Trent?" asked Jenny.

"Not much. But you know, I came across something interesting on my way up here today."

"How so?" asked Rod.

"We think we saw the reflection of a plane on the ground."

"You just saw a reflection?"

"Yeah. We couldn't see what it was because of the ground fog. But, I'm almost sure it was a plane."

"What color was it?"

"Silver. I'd bet it was a Cessna."

"What do you do when you see something like that, Trent?" asked Rod.

"Not too much you can do. I reported it to the FAA Flight Service Center in Anchorage, but they hadn't heard of anyone missing. There are no flight plans unaccounted for, so I told them I'd take another look tomorrow on our way back to Anchorage."

Then Jenny changed the subject.

"Trent, how long has it been since you lost your wife?"

"Five years. There's not a day goes by I don't think about it."

He was quiet a moment, and then said, "It's kind of like watching the lights of an airplane fly overhead in the night sky. As time passes, the plane is further and further away, and its lights become dimmer. But, in this case, it never completely disappears."

"We feel so bad for you."

"Don't. The pain is becoming less with each year that goes by. I enjoy my new life. What I do as a bush pilot is more useful than when I was working with the home builder in Seattle."

"Well, we sure appreciate all you've done for us," said Jenny.

"So, have you got any pelts for me to take back?"

"Yeah. There's a stack of seal skins and some otter skins," said Rod. "And could you believe it? One of the teenagers killed a polar bear. That skin is ready too."

"Okay. Maybe you can get some of your neighbors to put them in the plane," said Trent.

The money from pelts is what has kept everything going. Trent would take them to a broker in Anchorage, and then deposit the money into the village common account. The money paid for everything for the village and even provided for the grown kids to go to school. Most important to Trent, it paid for him to make these trips back and forth. The village elders made the decisions on dispersing the funds. Trent and other fliers were paid by them for taking the pelts out. Rod and Jenny were taken care of by their church in Seattle.

Jenny excused herself from the table, and called for a neighbor to organize the loading of the plane, and then she returned to the table to rejoin the conversation.

"That was a mighty fine stew you whipped up, Jenny," said Doc. "Now what were we eating?"

"Whale meat."

"Whale meat?" echoed Trent. "I thought whale meat was something like beef."

"It kind of looks like beef, but it's different."

"I hate to eat and run," said Trent, "But, we've got to get to Phelps Field before dark."

"Jenny," said Doc, "let's take a few minutes in the bedroom so we can see how your baby's coming along."

"Let's walk out to the plane, Trent, and make sure your load is secure," said Rod.

Flight to Fairbanks

"Remember what I said, Jenny. If you have any problems, or if you get anxious, send me a radio message and we'll come out to get you," said Doc, as he was about to climb into the Cessna. "You're carrying a healthy baby and we don't want anything to go wrong."

"Don't worry, Doc."

"I'll see you in a couple of weeks," said Trent, climbing through the plane's left door.

He started the engine, and with waves from Rod and Jenny, taxied to the edge of the landing area. He checked out the engine and the flight controls as he taxied, and turned the plane into what little wind there was. He pushed the throttle all the way forward, and waved at Jenny and Rod one last time. They were quickly airborne, and set their course to Fairbanks.

He contacted the Fairbanks Control Center, and filed his flight plan. The flight was uneventful, and when he sighted Phelps Field, he closed his plan, and lined up on the runway. The big broad flaps of the Cessna brought them down quickly, and when his skis touched the runway, he kept about half power on the engine and slid up to the gas pump.

"Well, Doc, we made it, and we didn't even crash," he teased.

"Pure luck," said Doc. "It's starting to get dark and you're low on fuel."

They took their overnight bags out of the back seat of the plane, and walked into the office.

Franklin, the office manager was just finishing business with another customer, when he turned and greeted Trent and Doc.

"Hi, Trent," said Franklin with a smile. He was a large husky man of about fifty years, and he'd been running the business as long as Trent had been coming in to the field.

"Hi, Frank."

"I'll be with you in just a minute."

"Take your time."

Franklin was just finishing business with the other man, Harold Fishman, on refueling and overnight tie down for his Bonanza.

"OK, Trent. You want gas and tie down for tonight?"

"Yep."

"I just called a cab for Harold, maybe you guys could share?"

The three men shook hands and greeted each other.

"Where you going, Harold?"

"Polaris Hotel."

"Yeah? We are too."

"I'll take care of your plane, Trent. We can settle up tomorrow," said Franklin.

"Hey, Frank. Have you heard of any missing planes lately?"

"No. Why?"

"I think I saw one on the ground about a hundred miles southwest of here. I think it was a Cessna."

"Jeez, there's tons of Cessnas in Alaska."

"Yeah, I know."

"In fact, your friend Ron Evans was in here a couple days ago, with his Cessna 180."

"I really don't know Ron that well. I've run into him from time to time."

"He came in here alone, but he must've scrounged up some business, 'cause he left here the next day with some dude, who wasn't from around here. This guy was sporting a rifle. They looked like they were going huntin'."

"Hunting? Now? It's a little out of season. Where were they going?"

"Beats me."

"Someone order a cab?" asked a cab driver, who just entered the door.

Mystery Man

On the ride into town, Trent learned Harold worked with a restaurant chain, and came to Fairbanks to help a new owner set up his business. He in turn, told Harold of some of his best adventures as a bush pilot.

"Actually," he explained, "the term 'bush pilot' is not what some fliers want to use anymore."

"Why is that?" asked, Harold.

"Because it connotes an image of reckless pilots flying antiquated planes. They now prefer to be called 'charter pilots' or 'contract pilots'."

"Well, that's what ya are," said Doc. "Reckless."

"C'mon, Doc," chided Trent.

Harold was amused over the bickering of the two men.

"I'd never ride with him if I didn't have to."

"Wadda ya mean, Doc? I'm a good pilot."

"I know ya are," said Doc, now serious. "You're the best. But, it's the chances ya take. It's gonna catch up with ya someday. I don't wanna be with you when it happens."

Trent was stung by his friend's honest feelings. It was no longer a joke. He thought about Martha, who had recently come into his life. They were co-owners of the Sky Harbor Inn, and close friends. Both of them had suffered a grievous loss, and were drawn to each other through this common bond. However, he knew his job was risky and did not want to put anyone through the grief he went through when he lost Anne to a terrible accident.

After he and Doc got settled in their hotel room, they went down to the first floor restaurant for dinner. Trent ordered his favorite, pan fried oysters with a Caesar Salad. After dinner he went to the bar and ordered a martini.

"Hi, Trent," greeted Charlie the bartender. He was a neat guy. Probably in his mid 30s, and was everyone's friend. Like most Alaskans, he was big and husky. No one argued with him if he cut them off for getting out of control.

"Hi, Charlie, what's been happening?"

"Nothin' new."

"Charlie, do you know Ron Evans?"

"Sure."

"Have you seen him lately?"

"Yeah. He was in here a couple of days ago. In fact he met someone here. Probably someone who wanted to go somewhere."

"Oh?"

"Yeah. He and some guy were sitting at that table over there, poring over a flight chart."

"Who was the guy?"

"I don't know. I think he's been staying here at the hotel for a few days. I'm sure he's from the lower forty-eight."

"What was he like?"

"He was probably in his forties. He said he was a trophy hunter, and he was showing around a picture album of animals. I remember him showing it to Ron. They were drinking and talking for hours. But, ya know, there was something about him."

"What do you mean?"

"I didn't like the guy. He was really arrogant. He reminded me of a 'Mafioso type'. Just being near him gave me a chill."

"Do you think he's still here?"

"I think he and Ron took off somewhere the next day. I haven't seen either one since that night. You know, Ron is just like you. He'll come in one day, stay the night, then he leaves the next day."

"Hmmm," Trent pondered.

After finishing his drink, he left the bar to go to his room. On the way, he stopped at the night desk.

"Hello, Sally."

"Hi, Trent," said a smiling young woman behind the desk.

"You got a guy staying here? About forty, probably from the states?"

"You mean the 'Great White Hunter'?"

"Wadda ya mean?"

"He's got an album of pictures of animals he's killed. He likes to brag about them."

"Is he around?"

"No. I think Ron Evans beat you out of a fare. They left here a couple of days ago. In fact I expected them back by yesterday."

"This guy got a name?"

"Let's see," she said as she scanned the register. "Here it is. Johnny D'Angelo. He said he used to be a prize fighter, but now he's a hunter."

"Johnny D'Angelo? Yeah, I remember him. He was a fighter, about twenty-five years ago."

"Is he famous?"

"Sort of. When he lost his title fight, he just disappeared. Some people think he lost on purpose."

"Really?"

"There was a big investigation accusing the Mafia of betting on the other guy, but nothing came of it." Trent slowly shook his head, "Wow! Did you see a rifle?"

"He had a gun case, or rifle sheath."

Blood on the Snow

Trent and Doc got up about seven o'clock, had breakfast and took a cab out to the airport. He settled with Franklin while Doc stowed their bags. After checking over his plane and verifying they had full tanks, they took off on a course to where they had seen a silver reflection on the day before.

"Fairbanks Center, Cessna 2446 Juliet would like to open a flight plan to Anchorage, with a possible stop enroute."

"Go ahead 46 Juliet."

Trent read off the required data to the controller, and then asked, "Do you have any unclosed flight plans from anyone leaving Fairbanks over the past few days?"

"No, is someone missing?"

"I'm not sure."

"You got a tail number or pilot name?"

"The pilot's name is Ron Evans."

"Negative. He didn't open one. Why are you asking?"

"I thought we saw a downed plane yesterday. If I see it again while going back to Anchorage, I might make a stop if I can."

"Let me know what you find."

"Roger."

Trent settled in for the hour's flight and watched the scenery on another perfectly clear morning. There was no fog this morning, so he was sure the mystery of what he saw the day before would likely be solved. But, he was anxious about what he might discover.

"Wadda ya think we're gonna find?" asked Doc.
"I think we're gonna find an airplane."
Doc looked worried.
"What's the matter, Doc?"
"I hate airplane crashes. Torn and burned bodies. God, they're terrible."

Doc had seen a number of them since living in Alaska. Weather caused most of them. He was often called to go in with recovery teams. He could never figure out why. He could never do anything about the carnage. But, he never refused to go.

Trent had seen his share of tragedies. The worst, of course, was the death of his wife five years earlier, caused by the propeller of his own plane while he was at the controls.

Now they were nearing the spot where they had seen the flash. Trent saw there was a frozen lake below them, and he could see something a few miles in front of him at its far edge.

"What's that?" said Doc.
"Where ya looking?"
"Right near the far shore of this lake."
He dropped down to a thousand feet above the icy surface.
"It's a plane!" cried Doc.
"Yeah, a Cessna 180."

He dropped down another five hundred feet and circled around the plane.

"It looks intact," said Trent. "It's no accident. It's an intentional landing. It looks like it's been taxied right up to the edge of the lake."

They could see the snow disturbed on both sides of the fuselage where two people had climbed out. The paths went beyond the front of the plane, up a draw, and over a slight ridge. Trent widened his circle to about a quarter mile radius from the Cessna. Now he could see beyond the ridge, where the terrain became a little flat valley.

"I see some objects."
"It looks like two butchered seals, from the blood on the snow," said Doc.

He knew they couldn't be seals. They were men. The third object was a rifle in the snow between them.

Trent climbed back up to a thousand feet over the lake and called Fairbanks Center.

"Fairbanks Center this is 46 Juliet, do you still have me on your radar scope?"

"Affirmative, 46 Juliet."

"Okay, I want to go ahead and close my flight plan for right now. I'm going to land here. I've found a plane on the ground."

"Roger. Do you see survivors?"

"It's not an accident, but it looks like there are two fatalities."

"Really? How did that happen?"

"I don't know, but I'm about to find out. I'm going to land on a frozen lake."

"OK, Juliet. We know where you are. Let us in on the story when you find out."

Trent throttled back when he was about over the middle of the lake. He made a wide gliding 180 degree turn, and lined up on the downed Cessna. He lowered the flaps, touched down and slid to a stop next to the other plane.

When they stepped out of his plane, they found their boots didn't sink too deeply into the snow. The cycles of thawing and re-freezing made a crust that could support their weight. He opened the baggage compartment and took out his .44 magnum. He checked to see that it was loaded, and then strapped it on his waist. He wasn't absolutely sure what had happened to those guys, but he had an idea, and he wasn't going up there without some protection.

Judgment

It was two days earlier that Ron Evans and Johnny D'Angelo landed on the frozen lake. They came there to kill a grizzly bear, still in hibernation. Ron was reluctant to be involved, but Johnny had plied him with liquor and put a five thousand dollar check in his hand.

"Every man has a price," Johnny had said, repeating an old cliché, "and yours was five grand."

They began walking slowly toward the den. Soon they could see the opening. It looked small because snow above it collapsed and partially filled it in. They stopped their advance about fifty feet from the opening. Johnny removed the camera strap from around his neck and gave it to Ron, who was right behind him.

"Here. All you have to do is point and shoot. It's all ready to go. I want you to snap the picture as soon as I fire."

Ron took the camera, and looped the strap around his neck. They again started slowly walking forward in a crouch. Johnny chambered a round in his rifle, and held it in a ready position.

"I don't think he's asleep. There are foot prints around the den," said Ron. "The breeze is at our backs. He knows we're here."

Now, they stopped just a few feet in front of the opening. Johnny looked back at Ron.

"Get that camera ready."

Suddenly, there was a brown explosion that burst out of the opening. Before Johnny could react, a huge paw, hit the left side of his head, breaking his neck instantly. Long claws drug across his face, ripping away flesh and his left eye. The force of the blow knocked him backward. His arms flew into the air launching his rifle, causing it to fly behind him.

When Ron heard the slap of the bear's paw, it was so loud he thought it was a rifle shot. He pushed the camera's shutter button, and caught a sight of gore. The bear then fell on him and sank its teeth into his lower jaw and throat. The bear returned to Johnny's body biting his face and crushed his head causing brain matter to spurt out.

Ron was not dead. His lower jaw was smashed, his throat was crushed, and nearly all of his ribs were broken. He could move his arms and hands. The camera was still strapped to his neck. He followed the strap with his hand until it reached the camera. His fingers could feel the shutter button. He couldn't lift the camera to his eye, but he was able to point it in the direction of the bear and Johnny, and snap the shutter.

The bear continued to rip and tear at the body. It was in a rage. It was as if it knew Johnny was the one that was going to do it harm. Finally, it stopped its rampage and sniffed the body. Then it walked away, out of the valley. Ron witnessed the whole ordeal, and then he died

Closure

It was easy for Trent and Doc to follow the trail, and it took about twenty minutes to reach the site. What they found when they got there was terrible.

The two men were lying on their backs. One's face was gone; eaten away. A great amount of blood stained the snow around his body. The other man's lower jaw and throat were crushed and torn.

Before them was what had obviously been a grizzly's hibernating den. Trent picked up the rifle, an 8 MM with a scope, with a bullet chambered, but it hadn't been fired. The first man's body was ten feet from the den opening. It was clear they were there to bag a hibernating bear.

The disturbed snow showed the bear had flown out from the opening, and caught the nearest man by surprise. The other man, who must have been Ron, was about ten feet behind the hunter. He had a Cannon 35 mm camera with a strap around his neck. Johnny must have given the camera to Ron so he could snap the picture of the kill. He probably had the camera up to his eye and didn't have a chance. Trent wondered if Ron maybe did snap a picture of the kill. Not the kill that was intended.

They thought about dragging the bodies down to the lake, and flying them out, then decided it would be better for the authorities to do all that. They might want to see the killing scene. They did take the men's wallets, camera and the rifle so some animal wouldn't drag them off.

Doc found a deposit receipt in Ron's pocket for five thousand dollars. Trent guessed it was the payment his fare had made for the flight. The receipt date was the same as Ron's flight, so he deposited the money before they left. Maybe he distrusted his passenger, and wanted to be sure the check was good.

They surveyed the scene once more before leaving. It was an open book. Ron left Fairbanks without a flight plan. The hunters had advanced on the den opening, as though they thought the bear would be cooperative, and calmly walk out. They got too close to the opening. It was clear the man with the rifle was trying to get an easy and illegal trophy. A picture of the killing shot was going to be taken by Ron.

Trent shook his head. He had never heard of anyone trying to kill a bear in this manner. Somehow, justice had been served. They returned to the lake, and opened the pilot's side door to Ron's Cessna 180, and placed the wallets and camera on the pilot's seat. Trent threw the rifle into the back seat.

"Well, Doc," said Trent, as he took one final look around. "Not much more we can do around here."

"What in the world were these guys thinking?" said Doc.

They manually swung the tail of the Cessna 185 around so the nose was pointed toward the opposite shore. Then they climbed in, started it up and took-off. After they were airborne, Trent resumed the heading for Anchorage. He picked up the mike and called Fairbanks Center.

"Fairbanks Center, this is Cessna 2446 Juliet."

"Go ahead 46 Juliet."

Trent recognized the voice as the controller he last talked with.

"Here's what we've found. Two men are dead from a bear mauling. You should call the State Police, and have them recover the bodies. Their Cessna 180 is on a nearby lake. I'm on my way to Anchorage, so please reactivate my flight plan. Over."

"Roger, 46 Juliet. I'm sorry to hear about the two guys. Have a safe flight home."